SONG OF THE SWORDS

Unto them will he come, son of Verdaine.
By the blood and the blade
of the one who is and who is not,
will the sacrifice be made.
Through Nadra's tears will the debt be paid.
Their majesty will once more be gained.
When the Prince of Dragons be named.
~ Second scroll, article nine of Verdaine's Prophecy

BOOKS BY TAMERI ETHERTON

Song of the Swords *

The Prince of Dragons

The Stones of Resurrection

The Temple of Sacrifice

The Ruins of Betrayal

The Veils of Deception

The Keeper of Stars

The Fatal Fae *

Fatal Illusion

Fatal Assassin

Fatal Legacy

Fatal Forever

Fatal Destiny

Court of Stars *

Sunset in Shadow

Chronicles of Eidyn *

Child of Fire

Dragon Mage

Daring Ever Afters *

Enchant

*Books that are part of the Aetherverse: The fantastical realms of Tameri Etherton. Characters and storylines intersect within the books with magical consequences.

This book is dedicated to my fabulous readers.
Without you, there would be no Aelinae.
Thank you for loving words as much as I do.
Truly. Madly. Deeply.

TEACUP
DRAGON
PUBLISHING

THE PRINCE OF DRAGONS

SONG OF THE SWORDS

TAMERI ETHERTON

AELINAE

WORLD MAP

N
THE WALL
THE NARTHVIER
LAN GYLLARELLE
MIDVALE
PADERAU
THE TELMARAN ISLANDS
SILIDEN R.
THE ULLAN DESERT
SEA OF JADEN
JADEN FLATS
ROAD
HIDDEN VALLEY
GREAT BARREN GORGE
ELDERS PASS
JANSEN STRAIT
ES OF AAR
JANSEN PLAIN
WASTES OF SLOE
THE EASTERN SEAS

Pendrian Wastes
Denk Scarbos
Western Seas
Caer Idris
Isle of Ardyn
Spine of Ohim
Caer Danuri
Mount Nadrene
Danuri Provence
Gaarendahl
Celyn Eryri
Talaith
Lake Oster
Ahkae
Summerlands
Stones of Kaldaar
Sitari
Summer Seas

The Narthvier
The Weirren
Lan Gyllarelle
The Ullan Desert
Telmaran Islands
Sea of Jaden
Paderau
Jansen Strait
Wastes of Sloe
Eastern Seas

THE TWO KINGDOMS
The Wall
The Narthvier
The Uttan Desert
Sea of Jaden
The Telmaran Islands
Great Barren Gorge
Jaden Flats
Hidden Valley
Jansen Strait
Elders Pass
Jansen Plain
Wastes of Sloe
Eastern Seas

THE SUMMER SEAS
MEKIAE
SRINIVAS
THATIRAKA
MNABAIE
SCIABARRA
DETARRE
AHKAE
SUMMERLANDS
ANTHOS
NYLS
SALDANNA
MENURRA
WINE FIELDS
PIRATES COVE
SITARI
The Sea Kingdom

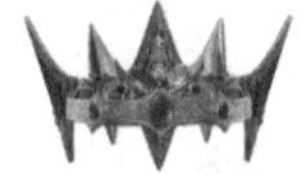

Be still, my love. Your wait is almost at an end.

Gilchrist settled his heavy body upon the sand, neither feeling its warmth nor noticing the tufts of dirt spiraling into the air. He sat motionless. Waiting. The voice stayed silent, yet he knew he'd heard his goddess. Knew what the message meant, yet he dared not hope the struggle his kind had faced for far too many seasons could be coming to a close. Behind him lay a wasteland that no longer kept them fed, no longer provided them with shelter from the constant ravages of wind. This place, this hell, had never been suitable for them and now his kind were dying. Each day brought a new challenge, another death. His aging heart couldn't bear one more loss.

Behind him lay death and suffering.

Before him, a large expanse of nothingness stretched to the shimmering veil that separated him from his home.

Aelinae.

How long had it been since he'd breathed the scent of fresh grass? How many seasons had they endured the scourge of this lifeless place? How many more would it take to annihilate them completely? These were the questions Gilchrist suffered alone.

The others looked to him for leadership. He could never give up believing in the words of the Caretakers. "We are one with the darathi," they'd said. "You shall never perish so long as even one of us lives." Yet where were they now? When Gilchrist and the others needed them so desperately?

A movement at his side drew his attention. "What brings you here today, Ahmbra?"

The youngling crouched beside him, her golden scales reflecting the morning sun. "Why do you sit here day after day? Why do you stare at nothing?" She lifted her wings against a breeze and snuffled into the dust. "What is so captivating about this canyon or the rocks below? They are the same as they were yesterday and the day before. Dull. Lifeless. Boring."

Gilchrist's heavy sigh died upon still air. "True, everything is as it has been for centuries. You were born here, young one. You do not understand what we lost." Ahmbra's birth had been a joyous occasion for the darathi vorsi. More than just a dragon born in exile, her birth had signaled a renewal of sorts—if they could survive this world's hostile environment, there was hope for them yet. They must keep believing.

Talons scratched across the sand as another dragon joined them. His mate, his love, his lifeblood.

"There are so few of us left. I do not believe she will ever see our homeland."

Jinnipher's words hung between them. She was right. Where once they were a proud race of thousands, they now numbered less than two hundred. They were the mighty darathi vorsi, air dragons born of the terrarae and stars. Their cousins, the darathi eneari, dwelled in the seas, but Gilchrist had not seen them for many seasons. He could only hope they survived the purge. A strange spiking cut at his heart. Like someone jabbing a talon between his scales to reach that soft spot in his chest. Tears scratched the backs of his eyes as he cast his mind to that day in the far too distant past.

A great war had raged between the gods, and the darathi vorsi were summoned to fight alongside their Caretakers. That day, they were betrayed by one of their own. How they didn't see Mallaqai's treachery sooner, he often contemplated. She was a sorceress, yes, but she'd also been a Changeling. One of the rare Aelans who could transform into a dragon.

Mallaqai had called them that day, not to lead or instruct or assist, but to trick them. His heart stuttered as he recalled the vortex she'd created, using the terrible power she'd stolen from the Lady of Light. Mallaqai should never have been able to control the weather, but that day she had. It was a miracle, Gilchrist and his brethren had thought. But no, it was not a miracle. It was theft on a grand scale, used to destroy the Aelans fighting against their god. That was long past and Gilchrist could no longer recall all of the events leading to the Great War, but of Mallaqai's betrayal, that was as fresh as a moment past.

"Come," Mallaqai had implored, "come near and you shall behold the destruction of Rykoto. We shall be victorious, but you must fly through this maelstrom to your destiny!"

They'd all believed her—Gilchrist, Jinnipher, and the others. Even the Caretakers who rode atop the great beasts had believed her, so pure was their desire to see evil banished. Yet they'd been led into a trap.

The vortex did not take them to the battlefield where Rykoto eventually lost the war, but to another world covered in dust, nearly devoid of life.

The Caretakers perished first. The heat of this world combined with lack of adequate food and water was too much for their tender hearts and soft flesh. Then, over the centuries, more darathi wasted to nothing, their bones becoming the dust upon which Gilchrist now rested.

The elder dragon peered once more into the misty veil, looking beyond the trees. Of all the darathi left, he was the only one who could see past the barrier that kept them locked in this hell. He alone suffered the yearning that glimpsing what was denied them brought.

"What is there?" Ahmbra's eyes were alight with mischief.

Yes, Gilchrist thought, *what is there?* Would it be the same as he remembered? Glens of wildflowers, mountains that stretched to tickle the sky, oceans the colors of jewels—did they remain? He could only see trees and, occasionally, the people who dwelled within the leafy cathedrals. The Caretakers. They had forsaken the darathi vorsi, it appeared. Not for a long time had anyone come through the mist, and he feared they never would. Yet fear led to their destruction and he would not let it claim his heart.

"Life," Gilchrist finally answered, rallying his enthusiasm for the youngling.

A movement beyond the veil caught his attention, and his scales vibrated with renewed tension.

"What is it, my love?" Jinnipher's wing tip scraped down his back, the touch soothing him.

He stared into the mist, fascinated and more than a little alarmed. Even Ahmbra sensed his excitement, for she trembled beside him, her scales fluttering in waves.

"I see our future. Our salvation." His long snout pulled into an awkward grin. A surge of suppressed expectation raced through his veins. Hope—something he'd tenuously held onto—stretched between his world and Aelinae. The words of the ancients at last were coming true.

Long ago, before the Great War and their banishment, before even Gilchrist had been hatched, there was an oracle who spoke of a time when Aelinae would suffer a great unbalance. It would take an anomaly, the oracle had said, to restore harmony. But this anomaly, one of the land but not of the world, couldn't save Aelinae alone. The darathi would play a role in bringing equilibrium to Aelinae and to do so, they needed a leader. Gilchrist had heard the tales and committed them to memory. He knew he'd have need of them later, and until such a time he must be patient.

At long last, it was time. The sign he'd been waiting for all those long seasons shone like a beacon through the veil.

He only wished the others could see it. Could see their salvation in the form of a tiny babe, one who would someday change the course of Aelinae and all who dwelled there. One who would walk between worlds and command darathi like his ancestors had once done. One who would not only be a Caretaker, but one of them—a darathi vorsi to rule all darathi. A son of the terrarae who controlled the sky.

He raised his face and tracked the beacon of light that shone from beyond the veil to a star just behind a dusky nebula. Silently, he gave thanks to his goddess before turning to face Ahmbra. She would soon know the importance of the words he next spoke. They all would. For with these words, the worlds would forever be altered.

"I see the birth of the Darathi Vorsi Prince."

The Prince of Dragons. Their exile would soon be at an end.

CHAPTER ONE

Sheanna. The word curdled his innards, twisted his veins until no blood flowed. His youthful heart pumped faster, searching for strength that was not there.

Surely she wasn't serious. Rhoane, a prince and First Son of the Eleri, sheanna. An outcast from his home, his family, his people. He'd never been beyond the third veil, and yet his mother, Queen Aislinn, expected him to live among the Fadair— not as one of them, but among them as if he were a part of their filth, their repugnant customs and traditions.

No. He couldn't do it. Wouldn't leave his family for an oath he'd made when he still wore short pants.

"Dance with me, my First Son. I can see by your furrowed brow you are upset with my request."

Rhoane glared at his mother, putting all of his angst into that one look. "Request? I seem to recall it more a royal command."

"You misinterpret my words, darling." They spun into the crowd, their voices lost to the din of chatter among the partygoers. This night they celebrated Carga's initiation as apprentice to their high priestess. It was not a night meant for family quarrels.

"You cannot stay here and wait for the Darennsai to find you. You must find her." A chill of warning bit against every syllable.

"What if Verdaine is wrong?"

Aislinn placed a cool palm upon his cheek. Her power thrummed below the surface of her skin, tempered but vast in its scope. There was no warmth in her touch, no gentleness in her words. "A goddess is rarely wrong."

Rarely, yes. Which meant there was the slight possibility she was wrong *this* time. But Rhoane wouldn't argue further with his mother. It was Carga's night, and he was determined to show his sister how proud of her he was. When the dance ended, he bowed low to his mother, then faced the dais, where his father sat on his imposing throne. They nodded a greeting to each other, and Rhoane excused himself to find Carga.

She stood with a group of young women, all dressed in long, filmy skirts and short, midriff-baring tops. Jewels glinted from the garments, sewn into delicate patterns of hummingbirds or flowers, depending on the maiden's preference. They wore their hair in long braids nearly touching their buttocks. Rhoane gave them all an appraising glance and ignored the more suggestive smiles directed to him. None of them knew he was promised to another. A Fadair. A woman without Eleri blood in her veins, who would one day destroy them all.

"Brother, is there something you wish to say?" Carga teased. "Or did you simply want to stare at these lovely creatures?"

Rhoane jerked his attention away from a particularly pretty girl's chest and cleared his throat. "I was hoping you would join me in a dance." Without waiting for an answer, he held out his arm for Carga.

She shrugged an apology to her friends and smiled sweetly at her brother. "What has you agitated this night? Now hush. I can see from your expression something is vexing you, and I know for fact it is not one of those ladies we just left."

Carga always had a way of cutting to the core of his thoughts. All his kind had the ability to connect to all Eleri, as if they shared a collective conscious, but Carga was able from a very young age to tap into their thoughts, to communicate with them directly. Living or dead, and even not yet born, she could call upon them for wisdom and advice, sometimes even to direct the events of the future. It was this uncanny ability, and her extraordinary skill with ShantiMari, that made her a candidate for high priestess. But first she had to complete her novice training.

Rhoane shut off his mind, even though she'd not tried to pry into his secrets. "I am fine, dear sister. Just tired from all the training Father is putting me through."

"He expects you to be a great leader. It is necessary, First Son of the Eleri."

Rhoane slid a glance to his brother, Bressal. Someday he would rule the Narthvier, the forest kingdom the Eleri called home. It was Rhoane's birthright as First Son to rule, but kingship was denied to him. Bitterness crept around his thoughts. "Let us not speak of that. Tell me, are you happy, Carga?"

Her eyes shone as she answered. "Desperately so. As you have trained your whole life to rule, I have spent my entire life preparing for tonight. That Verdaine saw fit to choose me at such a young age, I am honored beyond compare."

"You will be a wonderful priestess. Verdaine is lucky to have someone as devoted as you." He reached into his tunic pocket and withdrew a snippet of wood. On it, he'd carved the symbol for the trinity of power: Eleri, Light, and Dark. Some saw a single triangle with a swirling, continuous line from one corner to the next. Others saw three triangles interconnected. Still more saw a heart within the webbed design. Rhoane saw an elegant symbol that expressed the importance of each strain of ShantiMari. A simple reminder the three made up the whole.

Tears shimmered in her green eyes, turning them the shade of new moss. "This is lovely, thank you." She rolled the talisman over in her hand. "I can sense your ShantiMari within. You have infused it with a powerful spell of protection."

He hid his surprise with a cocky grin. "How do you know I did not supplant a spell of compelling into the wood? Then I could make you stay. With you gone to study at the temple, I will lose my fiercest competitor at cards."

"Your future is far from the gaming table, I am afraid." Her eyes grew misty, and she looked through him to another time, another place. "You will soon leave the vier. I see much redness surrounding you. Not blood. Anger." She blinked and glanced up to meet his steady gaze. "Is this true? Are you to leave us?"

Rhoane brushed her forehead with his lips, cursing the premonition that came with her enhanced power. "No. I am not leaving the Weirren. This is my home, my family. I will never forsake them."

"Nor will they forsake you. But you will leave, Rhoane. Sooner rather than later."

His gaze drifted to settle on his mother. She eyed him steadily as she sat on the dais beside her husband. Sadness clung to her frame, tugging her shoulders forward, her smile down. A lone tear glistened on her cheek.

"Then let it be later," Rhoane said. "Tonight, I wish to dance with my favorite sister before she abandons us for her duties."

Carga slapped his arm in a playful manner. "What has you so morbid? Truly, Rhoane, this is unlike you."

He spun her into the dance and forced a smile to curl his lips. For the next several bells, he didn't mention leaving the vier, nor did he let his mother's words upset his evening.

IT WASN'T until the next morning he discovered his sister had not been fooled.

Carga arrived at his door before the birds began their morning greetings. In her hands, she held a tray overflowing with plentas—pastry stuffed with sausage and cheese—berries swimming in a bowl of fresh cream, and two steaming mugs of grhom, the thick, spicy drink Eleri consumed for nearly every occasion. Rarely did Eleri drink wine, and only if grhom was not available. Rhoane's stomach gave an appreciative growl.

Carga glided past him into his room and set the tray on his desk, not bothering to move the papers scattered across the top. She turned to him, hands on hips, her face set. "Before you take one taste of this meal I have prepared specially for you, you will tell me what was bothering you last night. Do not try to lie to me, or I will remove this tray and never speak to you again."

He stifled a laugh at her dramatics. She always knew how to get what she wanted. "Fine, I will tell you, but you must promise to tell no one. Do I have your word?"

A dark brow arched over one of her lovely jade-green eyes and studied his features a moment before nodding. "I give you my word." She kissed her thumb before she touched it to her forehead and then her heart.

Rhoane let out a deep breath and sank into his desk chair. Words scurried through his mind, jumping from one thought to the next, never landing on any one idea long enough to form a coherent sentence. She'd warned him not to eat before telling her the truth, but the spicy sharpness of her grhom teased him. Courting her ire, he reached for a mug with one hand, a plenta with the other. He devoured the pastry in two bites. Carga studied him with practiced patience, her fingertips tapping along her crossed arms. After a long drink of grhom, he leaned back.

"When I was a young lad, too young really to understand what I was doing, Verdaine bound me to an oath. There would be a woman, she'd said, born to the Fadair, who would possess special powers. This woman would destroy the Eleri, but save Aelinae."

Rhoane left out the bulk of what Verdaine had told him that day long, long ago, choosing instead to give Carga the truncated story. He didn't much like recalling the words Verdaine had spoken, or the seriousness of her features. She'd terrified him, not by what she'd said, but by the fear he'd spied hidden deep in her eyes.

Despite his reluctance, Rhoane remembered the day with acute clarity. The way the leaves had rustled in the trees with dark solemnity, unlike most days, when their music was lighter, full of promise. The trees had understood the magnitude of his oath, even if he had not. He'd wanted to please his goddess, to see the furrowed brow etched across her beauty like a scar won in battle erased. Oh, how he recalled wanting to be favored by her, as if he alone could bring her happiness. It was too much for a small boy to comprehend, but Rhoane had agreed immediately to her demands. He would've promised her anything if only to see her smile once more.

"What of the woman, Rhoane?" Carga prompted, and Rhoane returned his focus to the present.

"Verdaine told me I would be the woman's life mate. She was my intended, and I would know no other but her."

Carga's eyes widened, and she whistled. "So, Verdaine sentenced you to becoming sheanna?"

"Yes, but that is not all. She told me the day would come when I would leave the vier to live among the Fadair. As an outcast from my home, I would be accepted into their lives with disgrace hanging above my name. Last night, Mother informed me the time has come."

Tears shimmered in Carga's eyes. "If Verdaine commands it, you must obey."

Rhoane didn't reply. It wasn't a matter of not obeying his

goddess. If the woman in question was Eleri, he'd have no qualms about keeping his promise, but the Fadair weren't Eleri. They were lesser beings who didn't understand his people or their ways. The Eleri kept apart from the rest of Aelinae for good reason—they had to keep their bloodlines pure to protect their power.

"Rhoane," Carga interrupted his thoughts, "you need to do this." She worried her thumbnail, tearing at the skin with her teeth.

It was Rhoane's turn to raise an eyebrow. Carga rarely gave away her nerves, even when confronted by their father's anger, which could be tremendous.

"I have read Verdaine's prophecy, in secret," Carga confessed. "I know I wasn't supposed to, but there are so many scrolls at the temple and this particular one was kept locked. I had to know what was within, so I bribed one of the keepers to let me see it. Even though I was a novice, she respected the fact I was a princess and, well, other things, and she let me take the scrolls for a few nights." Carga's green eyes flashed with a strange mischievousness he'd not seen from his sister before. Of the four royal children, she was the last one to suggest adventure or wickedness. "I know this—there is turmoil brewing beneath the surface of our world. The Eleri are not immune to the devastation the Fadair will cause." She paused, a crease marking her brow. "Never in my wildest imaginings did I consider the prophecy was about you. Why did you not tell me before now?"

"I did not want it to be true."

"You have read the prophecy, yes?"

He looked away, not wanting to meet her accusing stare. "I have skimmed it."

"Rhoane, this is serious. You cannot deny your place in our future. If the woman who can save us, save all of Aelinae, is a Fadair, so be it."

"No!" Rhoane slammed his mug on the desk. Grhom sloshed

over his papers. "Why would Verdaine punish me? Punish all Eleri?"

"Oh, my sweet brother. You have been listening to Bressal and Father for too long. Eleri are special, yes, but we are not above any creatures on this terrarae."

He ran his hands through his hair, intentionally loosening several braids. Carga tsk-tsked him and began to tighten the mess. He knew his sister well. She'd never been able to keep her fingers still if there was a braid needing repair. He wasn't ashamed to admit, on more than one occasion, he'd used the ruse to divert her anger.

Her fingers laced his tresses with expert precision. The familiar tug and smoothing calmed his racing heart, cleared his mind.

"I do not understand why a goddess needs a prophecy." It was something he'd pondered many times over the seasons. Certainly gods knew the future.

"It is not technically Verdaine's," Carga began. The crispness to her tone set him on alert. "The young woman who uttered the words was an ill-educated farm girl living near Lake Eion." When Rhoane jerked to look at her, she tugged hard on his braid, and he bit back the scornful comment. "Yes, an Aelan. She went into a trance, which frightened the dickens out of her father, and babbled about the destruction of Aelinae. Her father, not much better educated than she, called for the town cleric, who happened to be visiting a neighboring farm. He was able to write down every word."

"How fortuitous for them," Rhoane drawled as Carga finished her work and sat on the edge of a chair, arms folded across her chest. "Has it ever occurred to you they made it up?"

"Yes, it has. In fact, it occurred to several people. Until five other instances all across Aelinae were discovered where a young maiden went into a trance, said nearly word for word the same thing, and then fell over dead."

"They all died?"

"They call it Verdaine's prophecy because each girl said Verdaine's name. No other gods or goddesses were mentioned. Only our goddess."

"How terrible for the young women." Rhoane had never heard that part of the tale. He'd believed all this time Verdaine wrote the prophecy. "I suppose that changes things."

"Does this mean you accept what must be done?" a lyrical voice questioned from behind him.

Rhoane and Carga shared a look of surprise and turned to greet their goddess, Verdaine. Carga curtseyed nearly to the floor, her face a deep scarlet. Rhoane bowed low, as was expected.

"Welcome, Holy One. We are honored by your presence." He straightened, instinctively searching her eyes for any sign of worry. Joy filled them and he sighed with relief. He was not yet ready to leave his home.

Verdaine floated toward them. Her rust, olive, and golden hair hovered around her shoulders like a frame of forest. "I have come to fetch you, my young apprentice. When I did not find you in your rooms, I followed the sound of your voice. This conversation has been most stimulating."

Heat flared up Rhoane's neck. Perhaps he was mistaken and Verdaine was here to force him into honoring his oath. If so, he would refuse. He must stay to care for his mother and siblings, especially with Carga leaving the Weirren.

Verdaine swept her fingertips across his cheek and calm flowed through his veins. "I will not force you to do anything. You will know when it is time for you to honor your oath."

He shut his thoughts off from the goddess and her lips lifted in a smile. At least while he was able, he would have control of his life. "Will you come for me then, too?"

A sword appeared in her hand. Its long blade glowed white with ancient power that pulsed against his own ShantiMari. The dragon-scaled hilt fanned into a cross guard with intricately etched vines and designs unlike any he'd ever seen. A second, smaller guard flared to pointed ends. The blade—lithe, elegant, and lethal—stretched to a point. Words in a script he couldn't read wound their way up its polished surface.

"This will tell you when it is time. Take it, Rhoane."

"I cannot," he said. "This is a blade worthy of a god. No mortal should carry such a work of art."

Verdaine placed the sword in his hands. A smile further illuminated her beauty. "He was forged by your Artagh brothers after they left the vier. My father commissioned he be made for me, to fight in the Great War, but I couldn't bring myself to use it. When I refused, my father told me to keep him safe, that someday I would have need of him again. Not for myself, but for the one who would come from the terrarae."

"He?" Rhoane gripped the hilt hard, trying his best not to let the immense power of the sword overwhelm him. A song played in his mind. A joyful tune of remembrance. The sword welcomed him. No, it remembered him. Eyes wide, he glanced to his goddess.

"He and his mate were forged at the same time, with the same godsteel by twin Artagh. They are the rarest weapons on this world, with very special powers of their own." Verdaine ran a fingertip along the gleaming blade and more inscriptions became visible, only to disappear a moment later. "Claidholm Solais was forged for my use," she said, "but he was never truly mine. You are the only master this sword will know."

"Kleeve Solish?" Rhoane wrapped his lips around the strange name.

"Yes, Claidholm Solais. His name is derived from the old tongue. Listen well to his words. He will guide you to find the Darennsai. She will be known by her own sword, Ynyd Eirathnacht, the mate to this blade."

"The sword your father made for Daknys," Carga offered.

"No one has seen it since Rykoto was imprisoned. Many believe he destroyed the weapon during the fighting."

Verdaine's laughter was like the tinkling of small bells on a summer's breeze. "Ynyd Eirathnacht is not missing. She is safely guarded. When the time comes, Nadra will present her to the Darennsai."

"I would love to one day meet our Mother Goddess Nadra and her consort, our Great Father Ohlin. They so rarely show themselves. In fact, I cannot recall a time in our present history when they have," Carga said dreamily.

"Stop mooning over them," Rhoane chided. "It is juvenile and beneath you." He honestly couldn't understand his sister's fascination with the gods or the history of Aelinae. From his experience, he only saw the meddling gods did in their lives. The less gods he met, the better.

"Ignore your brother. Someday you shall have reason to know all the gods and goddesses, child." Verdaine touched Carga's cheek. "You will be my high priestess, after all." She returned her gaze to Rhoane. "You, too, will have reason to know not only my family, but our history as well. As I mentioned, this sword and Ynyd Eirathnacht are made of godsteel. You cannot destroy them. Not by fire, nor ShantiMari. The only way these two swords can be damaged is if they are used against each other in battle. They were made for peace, but must be united as one."

Rhoane held the sword close to his face and inspected the scrolling words. "What does it say?"

"That is for you to discover. I will only tell you this—if you and the Darennsai are not united as well, she will fail."

Rhoane recalled Verdaine saying something similar on the day he'd sworn his oath. Her life, he remembered thinking, was dependent upon his faithfulness. It was a terrible commitment to ask of any child.

"May I?" Carga held her hand out for the sword.

Rhoane cast a questioning glance to Verdaine. At her nod, he gently placed the blade upon Carga's palms. The glow diminished until the metal was cool and grey.

"Claidholm Solais, protect my brother when he journeys forth. Be as a guide to him when he is lost, a friend to him when he is lonely, and always, a reminder to him of his importance not just to the Eleri, but to all of Aelinae." The sword flared anew. Its brightness flooded his room with multihued streaks of light. "Claidholm Solais, Sword of Light." She breathed the final words upon the blade, and the rainbow dimmed to dull grey once more. Carga placed his fingers firmly around the hilt. Their power mingled with Claidholm Solais's. Light, Dark, and Eleri fused as one.

"Thank you," he whispered, and she grinned cheekily at him.

"Are you ready, Carga?" Verdaine hovered beside his sister.

Carga's eyes were alight with eagerness. Not an ounce of sadness marred their beauty. She was keen to leave the Weirren and begin her training. It was an excitement he couldn't share. "I would like to say my final farewells to my family, please."

Verdaine nodded and Carga sped from the room.

"When the time comes, you will be needing this as well," Verdaine said to Rhoane. A delicate silver chain with an unusual charm dangled from her fingertips. "This cynfar is for the Darennsai. A talisman, of sorts."

Rhoane took the pendant from his goddess and placed it in a drawer without looking too closely at the design. The less real he made the Darennsai, the more he could deny his oath.

"You will not always be able to hide that which brings you discomfort."

"I was young. Too young to make that oath and you know it. I should not have to honor it now that I understand the entirety of what I promised."

The worry he'd hoped to never see lurking in her eyes again bore straight to his heart.

"I had hoped, after all this time, you would come to see your oath not as a burden, but as a gift."

Rage stifled his breath. "A gift? To be sheanna? To be exiled from my family for what? Some girl who you say will destroy the Eleri? I am to give up all I have ever known and loved for someone who will bring an end to everything I have given up. Not only are you sentencing me to be an outcast in a hostile world, but you are asking me to condone the destruction of my people. If I honor this oath, I am condemning them all to a fate much worse than mine. I am guaranteeing their deaths."

"I admire your passion, Rhoane. Seasons change, tides ebb and flow. We cannot know the future until it happens." She hovered close enough he could see roots where veins should have been, smelled the musty scent of soil as if it were a perfume she wore. "Words are a funny thing. They are forever evolving in meaning and direction. Learn the words. Only then will you know your true course."

Her lips brushed his forehead and for one instant, he saw the clarity of the words inscribed upon his sword, then they were gone.

Carga burst into his room, her face beaming. "I have said my goodbyes. We can go now."

"Not yet." Rhoane folded his sister in his arms and held her a little too tightly. She squirmed, but he refused to let go. In truth, he admired her desire to seek a higher path. The Weirren stifled her, but not Rhoane. He needed nothing more than to be near the great tree and all who resided beneath its branches. This was home. "I will miss you."

"And I you." She pulled out from his grasp and held his face to hers, pulling him down until he was level with her. Their foreheads touched and she said, "When next we meet, may it be in sweetness and not sorrow."

"When next we meet," he finished the saying.

Long after Carga and Verdaine had left his rooms, he

wrapped Claidholm Solais in decorative coverings and muttered a ward of protection for the sword. He set it atop his dressing stand and sighed.

Even after this morning, he still wasn't sure he would honor his oath and leave the Narthvier.

A fancy sword wasn't enough to convince him a Fadair woman was worth the sacrifice.

CHAPTER TWO

Six moonturns passed before Rhoane thought again about the pendant. Each day he trained with Claidholm Solais, bettering his swordwork and learning the songs the sword sang, but came no closer to understanding their meaning. They were gibberish at best. The spoke of wars he'd never heard of, and histories not his. Sometimes, the sword sang of the Darennsai, but coded, as if it too were afraid of what she would become.

A fine Harvest morning shortly after his birthing day, he found the cynfar in his drawer, tucked into a corner amid the cruft of adolescent importance. His fingertips brushed the silver, and a jolt of power thrummed straight to his heart. He snatched his fingers from the offending metal and blew on them as if burned. When no blisters formed, he used the tip of his dagger to draw the necklace from its hiding place. A large diamond glittered from the center of a laurel wreath, and several smaller gems dotted a circle above the wreath. With his exhale, the leaves fluttered and he stared, mesmerized. The diamond caught the light and in its depths he saw a sphere, blue and green with wisps of white. He blinked and the vision disappeared, leaving the stone as unremarkable as an acorn.

It is time, Rhoane. Verdaine's voice whispered through the room on a gentle breeze.

"No," Rhoane argued aloud. A sense of foreboding overcame him, the same he felt each time he thought of abandoning his people. "I cannot leave the vier. Mother needs me, and Bressal is nowhere near ready to rule. I must stay."

Silence answered him.

He pushed the pendant to the back of the drawer and slammed it shut. He wasn't ready to leave. Not yet. If ever.

This would not do. He'd made the oath when he was too small to understand the magnitude of his promise. Surely his mother would agree with him now. If not her, his father, the king, could command him to stay. He would speak to the king presently and end this silly misunderstanding.

Rhoane grabbed his sword and strode to the inner courtyard, where his mother sat with her ladies-in-waiting, including Janeira, a warrior who had caught the eye of his brother. When Rhoane approached, Aislinn rose to greet him, but he stormed past without saying so much as hello.

"Prince Rhoane." Those two words froze his hurried pace. "What vexes you, my darling?"

"I cannot do it, Mother." He refused to look at her, to see the disappointment yet again in her eyes. "You need me. The vier needs me. This is my home, my people. I am their prince, their future king. How can I rule if I am off chasing a myth?" He grasped at his tattered reality, knowing his words were false. He was never meant to rule, never meant to sit on the Weirren Throne. He knew it in the marrow of his being, yet still he rejected his fate. "I was a child when I made that oath. I do not want to disappoint you or Verdaine, but I cannot leave."

"You can, and you must. We have discussed this."

"Mother, you are not being fair. Why me? Why not Bressal or Eoghan? Ferran's bells, Eoghan would love the opportunity to live outside the vier. Is it not possible to transfer my oath to him?

I am First Son. My duty is to the Weirren first, Verdaine second."

"You will do as told." Pale-blue veins rose on her forehead, a warning of her growing anger. In all the seasons he'd lived, rarely had he witnessed his mother losing her temper. Even on those few occasions, she'd remained in control, but this was different. The air snapped with her growing rage.

Rhoane took a step backward, and his mother shook her head in warning. Her arms stretched outward, fingers pointed directly at him.

"You will not run from me, boy. You were given this honor by our goddess. You not only disrespect her with your infantile whining, but you disrespect all Eleri." White flames danced along her arms and trailed from her long, ebony hair.

Fear seized him and he bent on one knee, head bowed. "I am sorry, Mother. Please, do not be upset. I will do as you ask."

His false, placating words did nothing. Her rage grew until she was covered in flames. Aislinn's power tugged at his own as she attempted to take what was not hers. Claidholm Solais sang a song of healing, but the queen was too far gone, her anger too rampant. Rhoane caressed the hilt of his weapon, unsure of how to stop his mother. This behavior was unlike the queen. A dangerous thought echoed through his mind. His mother acted not like herself, yet he knew it to be her. Therefore, she was creating this spectacle for no other reason than to frighten Rhoane. With a start, he realized the song was not meant for his mother, but for him.

Somewhere in the darkness of his spirit, he knew this was the only way. Aislinn understood Rhoane was beyond listening to reason and only an act of this magnitude would shake his core. Shame flooded his heart, drowning his denial, eradicating his self-righteous objections.

"What is happening here?" King Stephan burst through a door, bellowing to those in the courtyard. When he saw his wife engulfed in the deadly flames, he threw a blanket of his own ShantiMari over her. The flames snapped against his power, dissolving his threads to ash.

Aislinn held out her hand to her husband. "This is for the best. It must be done." Her voice lowered to a hush. "Husband, mi carae, you have my heart, always." She raised her head toward the sky and stole Claidholm Solais's power to her.

"Mother, do not do this!" Rhoane cried as the sword jerked against his grip. He fought against her power, his fist clenched protectively around the hilt. He struggled to stem the flood of light that infused his mother, but it was as if Claidholm Solais and the queen were determined in their efforts. *As if they'd planned it almost...* No. Rhoane wouldn't let the thought settle in his mind. Couldn't allow himself to believe such a terrible lie.

Aislinn screamed one ghastly, agonizing cry before she collapsed to the ground.

Stephan raced to her side and cradled her unmoving body against his. Tears streamed over his cheeks to drip onto his wife's pale face. The ladies-in-waiting twittered to one another, unsure of what they'd witnessed. They, too, sobbed.

Rhoane stood alone in the courtyard, grief making a statue of him. He neither cried nor wailed nor spoke. If this was a dream, he wanted it to end. But the nightmare was only just beginning.

Verdaine materialized in a haze of crimson, green, and gold. She spoke a few words to the Eleri king before she cradled the queen in her arms. "I will take her to Dal Tara, where she will reside with the other gods." Verdaine's glare cut Rhoane's heart. "Do not let her death be in vain."

His goddess rose slowly, and Rhoane mouthed the words, "I am sorry." To Verdaine or to his mother, he wasn't sure. If only he'd obeyed and done what they asked, his mother would be alive. If only he'd not been intent on defying his oath. *If only...*

Verdaine rose higher, her stare never leaving Rhoane. The last he saw of the women was nothing more than a spark of light against the verdant leaves of the Weirren.

King Stephan's chest heaved with his heavy breaths, and Rhoane braced himself for an outburst. Yet it did not come. What his father did say burned deeper than any accusation could.

"You are not to blame, my First Son. This horrific accident was not of your doing, nor of your mother's." His father paused. His brow made deep furrows in his usually smooth skin. "But you must leave the Narthvier this very day."

"She begged me, Father, but I did not listen." Rhoane collapsed in front of his father, his head bowed. "She told me it was time, but I was not ready. Despite your words, I will carry the shame of Mother's death until my own." Shame, hard and ragged and dark, pulled at his thoughts. His mother's death was his doing. Why his father chose not to blame him, he couldn't guess, but Rhoane would carry the guilt for the rest of his life.

His father eased Rhoane's sword from his clasped fingers. He didn't remember taking it from his scabbard.

"I am sorry," King Stephan whispered as he wound his son's hair around his fist. "Verdaine demands it."

With one slice of the blade, Rhoane's long, silky hair was shorn.

The ladies gasped. A few covered their faces and wept anew. Janeira advanced on her king. "My liege, it was not the prince's fault. The queen, she raged, but your son did not provoke the tragedy."

"Stay out of this, youngling. You know nothing of which you speak. Rhoane is sheanna and will live among the Fadair until such a time as he is fit to return." The entire time he spoke, Stephan's steady gaze never left Rhoane's. It burned to his center as surely as Verdaine's had. He'd lost his mother, his family, his home, and goddess because of his pride. Rhoane searched his father's eyes for even a tiny speck of hope and found none. The king's eyes were dark and impenetrable. A fresh wave of heartbreak washed over him.

"This is not how it is done," Janeira argued. "To become sheanna, there must be a council. He must be presented before the court so all will know his shame, but there is no fault here."

Stephan finally turned away from Rhoane, and a chill swept between them. "There is no shame present. No fault he must atone for. But Rhoane must be sheanna and leave the vier."

No shame, Rhoane thought, no fault? His mother was dead because of him, and yet the king said he bore no shame? Confusion silenced his tongue. His father was mad. That could be the only conclusion for him absolving Rhoane of the horrors they'd just witnessed.

"Why, Your Majesty? Why cast him out?" Janeira demanded. Few Eleri would stand up to the king and right then, Rhoane was grateful for the warrior.

Rhoane rose and looked Janeira full in the face. She met his gaze with a nod. In that small gesture, she said what Rhoane could not. He was sheanna. It didn't matter if he appreciated her arguments. His words would not be recognized at court until he was no longer exiled.

King Stephan stood and addressed those gathered in the courtyard. "Because," his low voice cracked, "he is *di diendum de la Darathi Vorsi di nobliesse Prientar.*"

He spoke in the language of the ancients, a dialect only a few Eleri understood, and even fewer could read or speak.

Janeira bent to one knee, her head bowed in supplication. "Forgive my impertinence, Your Highness."

Tears stung the backs of his eyes, but Rhoane would not disgrace himself further. His father had placed an even greater burden upon him. One he was not certain he deserved or could bear.

His father had named him the Dragon Prince—a title never claimed, never bestowed upon anyone before. As a child, Rhoane hadn't believed the stories his elders had told after supper in the great hall. How could one Eleri save an entire race of darathi on their own? For that's what all the tales foretold. One Eleri would reunite the darathi vorsi with the Caretakers—Rhoane's people. But how? The darathi were banished during the Great War. Some said it was a witch named Mallaqai who'd led the great beasts astray. Others claimed it had been the mad god Rykoto himself who'd rid Aelinae of all darathi, not just the vorsi. How could Rhoane be expected to find them and remain true to his oath? Rhoane slid Claidholm Solais into the scabbard, not yet ready to believe he was this fabled prince. Still unable to see his path.

Pale light glowed from the sword, illuminating the decorative leather that encased it. He placed his palm over the hilt and flinched at the tremor of power that stung his skin. What did it mean? What did any of this mean?

He bowed to his father and kissed his extended fingertips. Rhoane spoke no words, for all his emotions and thoughts were clouded with grief. His father's ShantiMari pulsed with his own, connecting them in a way no touch could. Rhoane experienced the king's heartache as if it were his own. Felt the raw anger Stephan had toward Verdaine. Before he did anything else rash, Rhoane severed the connection and strode away. He refused to meet the stares of the Eleri who'd gathered in the courtyard.

He was sheanna now. No longer one of them.

CHAPTER THREE

A fine mist curled at the edge of the road that led from the Weirren to beyond the veils. Shadows cloaked the trees, obscuring Rhoane's visibility. He strode with purpose, wanting nothing more than to leave the vier and his heartache behind. But he knew it wouldn't be so easy. Knew the image of his mother engulfed in flames would stay with him for eternity.

He tapped the pocket that held the cynfar. He'd dishonored his goddess once and would not fail her again. If the Darennsai lived among the Fadair, he would find her. Somehow, he would right the wrong of his mother's death. He'd been a lad when he made the oath, but he was no longer an innocent. He'd tried to break a promise made to his goddess and destroyed his mother. To make amends, he must accept his fate, even if it meant living the rest of his life away from his home. If the gods willed him to be the Darathi Vorsi Prince, the Prince of Dragons, so be it. It wouldn't diminish his shame, but it might help restore his honor. And in the process, mend his father's broken heart.

Claidholm Solais hummed in his mind, soothing notes of happier times. Memories of his childhood drifted through his thoughts. He patted the handle of his sword. A grim smile tightened his face. His pace increased, and he replayed the last conversations he'd had with Verdaine, his mother, and his sister. They believed in the prophecy. If he were to find the girl and right Aelinae's wrongs, he would have to believe in it as well. All of it, not just what suited him. Which meant he needed to fully read the scrolls. He'd not seen them since he was a lad, still in short pants and with few cares.

A rustling of leaves brought his attention to the path before him. The road was deserted, save for a few randy hares scampering into the ferns to his left. His hand hovered above the hilt of his sword. His pace slowed, and he peered deeper into the forest.

A slight figure emerged from the trees, and Rhoane jerked his sword from its scabbard. The blade was at the intruder's throat before either had a chance to speak.

"For Ohlin's sake, Rhoane!" Eoghan sputtered, his eyes wide. "I thought you might like a mount, and this is how you repay me?"

Rhoane recoiled at the sound of his brother's voice. "I thought you a brigand meant to rob me."

"If you are to survive the Fadair, you must not be so quick to kill." Eoghan indicated the blade a breath away from his skin. Rhoane lowered it with a mumbled apology. The long face of a horse rose above Eoghan's shoulder and he led her out of their hiding place. "She is the best I could smuggle out of Father's stables. She isn't fast or made for battle, but she will make your journey bearable until you can acquire a more fitting beast."

His youngest brother, sixty seasons his junior, was sometimes far wiser than even the elders of their clan. Rhoane had been mired in the darkest misery when he'd left the Weirren—it hadn't occurred to him to secure a ride. "Thank you, Eoghan." Rhoane gripped his brother's arm and pulled him into a bear hug. "I will miss you."

"And I you, First Son of the Eleri." Eoghan broke off the

embrace and indicated the stuffed saddlebags. "You have enough nourishment to last a fortnight, longer if you set traps."

"Again, I am indebted to you."

"You can repay me by not getting killed."

A second figure emerged from the forest, this time from the other side of the road. Rhoane shielded Eoghan and held his sword aloft.

"Will you murder your only sister?" Carga stepped lightly onto the dirt path and lowered Rhoane's sword with her fingertips. "Eoghan is right. You are too quick with the sword, and not with your mind." She glanced nervously at the road leading to the Weirren. "We do not have much time. Eoghan and I will escort you to the final veil." She withdrew a scroll from the folds of her gown and handed it to Rhoane. "I copied as many versions of the prophecy as I could. They keep us busy at the temple, but I knew you would need these. There is a complete translation in Talaith. The empress has an impressive library. Since you must present yourself to her as an Eleri noble anyway, you might as well make use of your time there."

"I must go to Talaith?" Rhoane asked. "Why not Haversham? Or the Summerlands?"

"You will travel to all seven kingdoms, dear brother, but I feel certain you will find your Darennsai in Talaith."

"Have you had a vision?" Eoghan's eyes sparkled like a forest pond.

"Nay, but I cannot shake the feeling Talaith plays an important role in all our lives."

They reached the final veil and paused. None of them were eager for what was to come, but Rhoane knew it was up to him to lift the last veil. Carga and Eoghan had done their part, and now he must journey alone.

"Be safe, Rhoane." Carga stretched to kiss his cheek, and he embraced his sister with a fierceness that surprised them both.

Eoghan wrapped his gangly arms around the pair and held firm. "I will miss our adventures."

"As will I." Rhoane rested his chin atop his younger brother's head. "I will miss everything about the vier and our lives. Nothing will ever be the same."

"Perhaps that is for the best," Carga murmured. "The Eleri are dying. Most only have one child—some none at all. Mother and Father were anomalies with four."

Rhoane tightened his grip, not wanting to let go. Not just yet.

"The Darennsai is not the destroyer of our race. She is the harbinger of something new and enlightening. She will bring peace to Aelinae and usher in a new way of life for everyone." Carga's dreamy, faraway tone was one Rhoane had learned to never question. Not often did she speak with foresight, but when she did, he listened.

Eoghan blinked twice and shook his head, his eyes filled with wild excitement. "I saw her."

"Who? The Darennsai? Where is she?" Carga's breathless words tumbled out.

"No, my life mate." A tremble started in Eoghan's legs and continued until his entire body shook. "With your words, I saw her."

"What did you see?" Rhoane steadied his brother, but the lad continued to quake. "Who is your life mate?"

"A vision. Perfection made in womanly form."

Carga slapped her younger brother's wrist and chuckled nervously. "You ass. Are you trying to frighten us with your contrived convulsing?"

Eoghan's trembling continued despite his jovial tone. "As are you with your mysterious proclamations, I would say. Besides, I could not let Rhoane have all the fun, now could I?" He stepped away from his older brother and did not meet his eyes.

Rhoane chuckled at the supposed quip, but Eoghan wasn't

one for dramatics. He believed his brother did have a vision and was frightened by its intensity. The desire to stay longer with his two closest confidants was powerful, but lingering would only delay the inevitable. "If there are no more revelations to be made, perhaps I should be on my way?"

They said their good-byes with well-wishes whispered and many extended embraces shared.

"Go now. I do not wish for you to see me through the veil," Rhoane commanded, his voice heavy with emotion. He waited until they'd walked along the path and could no longer be seen before he turned to the final veil and said the words that would allow him entry into the lands of the Fadair.

Although Rhoane was sheanna, he did not bear the taint others had in their exile. That small distinction did nothing to make the shame any less. He felt every sensation as if it were a torch held too close to his skin. In time, he would learn to control the agony, but for this morning, when he had to leave his family and beloved forest for a world he didn't know and wasn't sure he was welcome in, the pain was nearly unbearable.

Rhoane stood at the edge of trees that marked the boundary of the Narthvier and took a deep breath.

His first step onto Fadair soil was, well, unremarkable. Unsure what he'd expected, Rhoane stepped lightly across the glen, testing his weight against the soil. Nothing swallowed him whole, nor did monsters arrive to ravage him. The sky looked much the same as it had in the vier, but not obscured by leaves. The glens had no trees, and he was unrelentingly exposed in the wide-open land. That much space should have terrified him, but he found it strangely compelling.

For the better part of two bells, he left his mare to graze on the long grasses and investigated the tiny pockets of life that existed outside the forest. The same critters found in the vier scurried beneath bushes. Rodents of no particular interest made nests and burrows while birds darted across the cloudless sky.

The expanse of openness sprawled in every direction, and for a moment, terror seized him. He had no idea which way to travel first. From his childhood tutors, he recalled vague recollections of Aelinae's kingdoms. The Summerlands in the far south, past Talaith. The Ullans to the east, Artaghs to the southwest, Danuri on the western coast, Caer Idris to the north of Danuri, and the blue-skinned warrior women on an island somewhere in the Southern Seas.

Rhoane turned eastward toward Ulla. Renowned horsemen, the Ullans were far coarser than the fair folk of Talaith, and despite Carga's premonition that the Darennsai would be found to the south, he had need of the Ullans. He patted the mare's neck. Talaith would have to wait a few moonturns. He needed a sturdier mount who could handle all of the riding he'd be doing. The mare Eoghan smuggled out of their father's stables was too gentle and he feared couldn't handle the rigorous pace.

Once he reached Ulla's border, it became clear trading his mare wasn't going to be as easy as he'd hoped. His welcome into the desert kingdom came in the form of masked riders who circled him, their scythes held high, their calls like carlix screeches. Rhoane slowed his mount and took in the dark eyes that peeked through black fabric. Male or female, he couldn't tell, but their weapons looked deadly enough.

"You are not welcome, Aelan," one of the riders shouted at him in Elennish, the favored language of the Fadair. "Leave now."

"I am not Aelan," Rhoane began, unsure whether they would receive an Eleri over Aelan, but guessing not. "I am Prince Rhoane, First Son of the Eleri."

A nervous mumbling came from several of the Ullans. Finally, one rider broke from the circle and approached. Clad entirely in black from the top of their head to the tips of their boots, only a slice of tanned skin and eyes the color of melting ice could be seen. When their horse's snout stood even with his mare's, the rider addressed him. "You wear your hair short, exiled son of our neighbor. Follow me." The voice, decidedly feminine, brooked no argument.

The rider wheeled her horse around, and Rhoane followed, keeping watch on the others who continued to surround him. He was decent with a sword, but ten on one were not good odds for survival. They rode far into the desert, crossing patches of shifting sands and valleys with rock sculptures arching high above them. Rhoane marveled at the beauty of the harsh land. All shades of red, from deep rust to pale coral, were etched into the rocks. Black sands gave way to dazzling white shifts of gravel.

They climbed a steep ravine, and at the top, Rhoane saw a huge lake nestled against the border of the Narthvier. The Sea of Jaden. He'd heard tales of Eleri drowning in the sea to avoid their sheanna. He shuddered and looked away from the shimmering water. A city made of colorful tents rested at the base of the mountain. Hundreds of tiny pennants whipped against the winds that blew constantly across the sands.

"Is that where you are taking me?" Rhoane asked. It was the first time any of them had spoken since setting off.

The leader lifted her chin. "For now. The chief will decide what we should do with an Eleri exile."

Their horses scrambled down the mountainside with the grace and agility born of familiarity. His mare had neither the experience nor the youth needed to traverse the rocky path, and slipped every other step. Rhoane eventually dismounted and led his mare as best he could, choosing a goat path wherever possible. At last, he reached the bottom and solid ground. The mare nickered to him as he placed his head against her forelock, apologizing for the harrowing descent.

When he remounted, the leader watched him. A glint of something not completely unkind shone from her light eyes.

Several young boys came to take their mounts and Rhoane released his mare reluctantly. The Ullans were known for their horse skills, but would they treat a potential enemy's mare are well as their own? He hoped so.

The woman led him to a bright-yellow tent at the heart of the camp and paused before entering. Two massive guards wearing loose-fitting breeches and nothing on their heavily muscled torsos stepped aside to allow them passage. Rhoane was not overly tall for an Eleri, standing the height of a young sapling, but these men were another head and a half taller than him. As he passed, he studied their bald heads and thick arms, noting the intricate markings upon their skin. He'd never heard of Ullans being giants, and the woman who led them to the front of the tent looked no taller than his own sister.

Inside the tent, several Ullans stood in corners conversing, or sat upon cushions in small groups. None of them looked to be of the same bulk as the guards. Rhoane's anxiety lessened a notch.

The woman ignored everyone in the tent and stopped before a raised dais, where the Ullan chief rested atop thick pillows. For several moments he regarded them coolly, a pipe at his lips. After a hasty conversation in Ullan, the woman indicated Rhoane, then said in Elennish, "He says he is a prince of the Eleri." Her tone suggested she believed otherwise. "Known as Rhoane."

Without further introductions, she knelt at the side of the chief, who regarded Rhoane from where he reclined, not getting up to greet him, as was proper.

Rhoane bent low at the waist, affording the chief the greatest honor he knew. "I am Prince Rhoane of—"

"Why have you come to my kingdom?" The chief interrupted. His black eyes blazed as he took a slow drag from his pipe. Tendrils of smoke curled around the man's inscrutable gaze, yet he didn't blink. He, like many other men in the tent, did not wear a head covering.

Rhoane shifted from one foot to the other. Uncertainty settled in his gut. "I need a sturdy horse. One that will endure the riding I have before me."

"Ha!" the chief barked, and the others in the tent laughed with him. "You Eleri think you can stroll into the desert and the Ullans will just give you a horse." He leaned forward until Rhoane could smell the spicy scent of tobacco on his breath. "If you want a horse, you will have to earn it, boy."

Several times the chief glanced to his left, where the hooded rider sat motionless. A flash of eyes, darker in the tent, now clear blue like the waters from Lan Gyllarelle, gave Rhoane all the warning he needed.

"How does one earn a horse, my lord?" Rhoane bent to one knee, his head bowed in supplication. If the chief were power hungry, he'd not anger him by challenging his authority. An Eleri prince far outranked a simple Ullan chief, but though Rhoane was a prince in title, he was sheanna. If the chief demanded he work off the price of a horse, he would not shirk the duty.

"You entertain me." The chief cocked his head to the side. A sour grin marred his otherwise handsome features. "Although I doubt you will last long in the arena."

Hairs rose on the back of Rhoane's neck, and anxiety prickled against his skin. He'd heard tales of Ullan fights held in their arenas. Mostly between men and women convicted of crimes, but sometimes out of spite from their ruler.

"I have committed no crime. Why must I be subjected to your punishment?"

The figure to the chief's left glanced down, and Rhoane swallowed a lump of fear.

The chief's words were low, guttural. "Committed no crime? You entered Ullan territory without permission. You came here to steal a horse, and most likely also our women. I say you've committed several crimes, exiled son of Stephan."

"I did no such thing! You—" The woman shot him an alarmed look, and he stopped.

The chief glared at the figure to his left. "Kaleigh understands when to be silent and when to speak, don't you, my dove?"

"Yes, my lord." Kaleigh's eyes shone with adoration as she gazed at the chief. The lilt to her tone, however, set Rhoane further on edge. Kaleigh was not Ullan, of that he was certain. From her posture to the way her words caressed each syllable, he was almost certain she was one of his people.

"You accuse me of stealing women, and yet you have an Eleri held captive in this very tent?" Rage boiled through his veins, deafening him to the sounds outside the tent. Only the three of them existed.

"I am here of my own will, First Son." Kaleigh's calm, reassuring declaration sent his anger spiraling. Confusion clouded his judgment.

Rhoane glared at the chief, then at Kaleigh, looking to them for understanding. "But, why?"

His mind reeled with all that had happened in the space of a few bells. The world he knew had been turned upside down and twisted beyond recognition. He leaned back on his heels, kneeling where no prince should, and still pride would not let him accept defeat. His battered psyche couldn't take much more. It wasn't enough he'd already suffered his mother's death, being claimed sheanna, and losing his family and friends. Now he was to be held against his will. The culmination of events dragged his spirit to the depths of an unholy despair.

The chief regarded him with a mean glint to his eyes, a wolfish smile on his lips. "You are my prisoner, Eleri. You will fight in my arena, as all prisoners do. If you please me, you will be released."

A last shred of defiance rallied and Rhoane rose without being given permission. "Why am I your prisoner? I have committed no crime. I did not come here to steal a horse. I am more than willing to work for a mount, but I will not acquiesce to being your prisoner." Fresh rage coursed through him, but he tamped his ShantiMari down until it barely registered. He would not use his power, not here, not on this man. The flames on his mother's arms taunted him, teased him into submission. "I am the First Son of the Eleri. If you keep me here against my will, you will have war with my people."

Kaleigh's eyes tightened, but she did not speak up for Rhoane. He was her prince, and yet she forsake him for the chief. Hope began to fade from his thoughts. If the Ullan chief could keep an Eleri woman as prisoner with no one the wiser, how easy would it be to keep him here, too?

As if reading his mind, the chief said, "You wear your hair short, Eleri. That means you are exiled. I don't believe anyone will come looking for you, and I doubt there would be a war to reclaim you." His dark eyes flicked around the room to the men. "You could try to fight your way out, but it would only end in your death. You are my prisoner whether you want to accept it or not. There is only one way you can leave and that is through combat in my arena. Anyone who enters my lands without my permission is subject to the same law. Fight or die."

"If I fight, how long before I earn my freedom?"

The chief reclined against the cushions and sucked on his pipe. "When I decide."

Rhoane's hatred burned through him. Not only for the Ullan chief and his Eleri captive, but for the situation he found himself in. All of this for a horse. No, not just the horse—for a Fadair woman who would someday destroy his people. It wasn't worth it.

CHAPTER FOUR

While the tribe ate, Rhoane was forced to sit off to the side by himself, yet near enough he could hear everything the chief said. Forced to wait until the tribe was fed, with nothing being offered to him, an Eleri prince. On several occasions, the chief made sure he saw that Kaleigh had plenty. More than once, the chief fed the woman himself, placing a morsel of food between his lips and making her take the offering with her own.

Unending rage simmered beneath Rhoane's calm façade. Never in his life had he witnessed an Eleri woman be submissive to a man. It never occurred to him that women might enjoy giving their power to a mate. Unease coupled with curiosity made him study Kaleigh and the chief. She did not appear bothered by her station, nor did she give the impression she needed the chief's permission to come and go, as attested to by her leaving the tent twice during the meal. Neither occasion did she wait for the chief, instead she simply stood and walked away. Both times, the chief would turn to watch the Eleri woman, a smile upon his lips.

The relationship, puzzling as it was, could not keep Rhoane's mind fully off what was to come once the meal concluded. When the chief and Kaleigh finished eating, they rose from the mound of cushions. A guard poked the butt end of his spear against Rhoane's ribs and gave an order in Ullan that he didn't understand. Rhoane stood, half tempted to take the man's weapon and break it over his head. Instead, he silently followed the man to yet another tent, this one smaller and devoid of any decorative embellishments.

The chief met him there and proceeded to take all of Rhoane's weapons, including Claidholm Solais, which he wrapped in a thick sheep's hide.

"I urge you, sir, to not take that blade," Rhoane argued. "Allow me to keep it, even if locked in a trunk."

The chief snorted a laugh and ordered Rhoane to be restrained while the guards removed his possessions. His Shanti-Mari pressed against his control, begging to be unleashed, but he refused. Once again, the image of his mother engulfed in flames tempered his actions.

The sword sang in his mind, calming him, assuring him there was no danger of being confiscated for good. Rhoane wished he had the blade's confidence. He'd never fought without a weapon —for as long as he could remember, he'd had a sword or bow or staff at his disposal.

The group wove their way through the camp until they came to a large open area with wooden benches built into the hillside, giving the spectators an unobstructed view of the fighting area. Rhoane scanned the faces of the gathered Ullans. Most wore expectant smiles, with a few hiding their disgust. Interesting. Not all Ullans enjoyed the chief's entertainment. Rhoane tucked the knowledge away and focused on the large roped-off area where the fighting would take place.

In the center of the ring, a shaggy brute spun a dagger between his fingers.

"Why is he armed while I am denied weapons?"

"In the arena, weapons must be earned. Each contestant starts with exactly nothing. Winner takes all." A note similar to sadness echoed in Kaleigh's words. If Rhoane were to guess, she, too, did not enjoy the fights.

Rhoane was led to the center of the ring and left standing near his opponent. The man barely reached his chest; however, what he lacked in height, Rhoane soon discovered he made up for in speed. Rhoane had heard stories about huge lizard creatures called vorlocks and their riders. The man he fought had to be one of those men. He wore only leather breeches with bones knotted along the seams. No shirt, no shoes, and no armor. Only a thick coating of fur covered his square chest and bulky arms. The chief might've taken Rhoane's weapons, but at least he let Rhoane keep his clothing.

For near on half a bell, Rhoane struggled with the stocky man. He darted away from the man's dagger time and again, only to be bludgeoned with a shaggy fist. He began to see a pattern to the man's movements and tracked him like he would a doe. Dodging yet another swipe with the lethal dagger, Rhoane caught his opponent off guard and wrestled the slim weapon from his grip. In the melee, the blade slashed Rhoane's thigh before he maneuvered it to impale the vorlock rider.

A sickening squelch was the last sound the man made before he crumpled to the ground. Bile splashed against the roof of Rhoane's mouth but he did not look away. Would not give the chief the pleasure of seeing how much the man's death bothered him. He'd never killed before.

Blood stained the sand a deep shade of crimson. Rhoane wasn't sure how much had come from him or from his opponent. Lightheaded from lack of food and his exertion in defeating the vorlock rider, Rhoane stood on unsteady legs to face the chief.

Kaleigh remained sitting while the chief stood to applaud Rhoane. "A passable victory for a boy," he called out and Rhoane seethed anew.

The fight had been pointless. Empty entertainment for a stupid and vain ruler.

"My name," the chief said when he reached the ropes separating the arena from the seating area, "is Amdi Agnar. You may call me laird."

"I shall call you Lord Agnar, and you may call me Prince Rhoane."

The chief laughed and slapped Rhoane on the back. The blow forced much of the air from his lungs. It was all he could do not to sputter and cough. This was not the time to show weakness, if ever there was around the Ullan chief.

"We shall see, boy." Amdi had two soldiers escort Rhoane to a tent, where they stood beside the door, impassive and unmoving.

Food sat on a table and water steamed from a ceramic basin. Clean cloths rested beside the beautifully painted container. Rhoane stripped off his tunic and under shirt, grimacing at the amount of blood staining both. Several cuts marked his chest. Blood oozed from the slash on his thigh. The adrenaline rush he'd had in the arena passed and he struggled to remain standing. He focused on his task, pushing his exhaustion aside. With a damp cloth, he cleaned his wounds. Most were superficial, some deep enough to need stitching.

As he worked, he studied the details of the water container, admiring the flow of paint from one object to the next. The artist had depicted a scene of the desert with blooms dotting the landscape.

"So, there is beauty among the violence?" Rhoane's words, spoken in Eleri, floated on silence.

"You will find, Your Highness, there is much beauty here." Rhoane glanced up to find Kaleigh standing in shadows near the entrance to the tent. "Even with men as rough as Amdi." She approached and took the cloth from his trembling fingers. With deft precision, she applied pressure to the largest wound. "It would be best if you did not speak our native tongue here. They do not trust outsiders. I know you have questions. Ask them." Her Elennish was fluent, unlike his. He'd learned the language as he'd been taught, but didn't have much use for it growing up. Until now.

"Should I not have permission from your gaoler?"

"I am not a prisoner here." She removed the veil from her face, then carefully placed her elaborate headdress on a side table.

Rhoane sucked in a breath, not at her beauty, which was great, but at her hair. "You are sheanna. But how?" He broke all protocol by asking the simple question. Sheanna was not to be discussed unless the exiled Eleri chose to speak of it, but he had to know. Had to understand.

Kaleigh's short blonde curls bounced when she chuckled. "I fell in love. Before Amdi, before all of this." She indicated the tent and camp beyond. "Unfortunately, the woman did not love me in return." Rhoane winced as she pressed the cloth to an especially vicious cut. "I am sorry, my lord. Would you like me to stop?"

"Please, continue." He motioned to the water, but he meant her story. "And call me Rhoane. Here I am not a prince, it would seem, but a boy."

"You *are* a boy, Rhoane. In the Narthvier you are, what, one hundred seasons?"

"One hundred twenty-two."

"To the Fadair, that is equivalent to being twenty-two or twenty-three seasons." At his look of confusion, she continued. "Time does not move the same here as it does in the vier. I am three hundred fifty-nine seasons Eleri, but only sixty-four to these people. To them, I am an adult, but you are not yet. Not until you reach your thirty-fifth Aelan season."

"That is why the chief enjoys taunting me. To him, I am but an adolescent. He thinks to teach me a lesson, does he not?"

"Aye, he does. And you should pay attention to all he can give you, Prince Rhoane." She finished cleaning the worst of his wounds and applied a thick paste to them all. Her touch was light against his skin, as if she didn't want too much contact between them.

The absence of her touch was both a relief and a torment. It was not the first time someone had laid hands upon his flesh, but it was the first time he'd had any sort of reaction to a woman's touch. As if sensing his arousal, Kaleigh backed away to rinse her fingers in the bloodied water. Embarrassment and shame washed through his desire. He was promised to another. It wasn't right to notice the curve of her neck or the way her fingers danced upon his skin.

"You are young, Rhoane, and untested. Amdi can teach you many things you will need to survive with the Fadair." She met his gaze, and her startlingly blue eyes bore straight to his spirit, challenging. "Once you best the arena, I can show you how to manipulate time. Only a few Eleri know how, and before I was cast out, I was one of the best."

Rhoane took the plain tunic she offered and covered his naked torso. The salve stuck to the fabric, but he didn't care. It was better than standing half-naked in front of her.

"Why have I never heard of this before? I am skilled in Eleri healing, and I am one of the best with ShantiMari. Everyone says so."

"Because, my prince, only the initiates of Verdaine are taught the ways of time."

Rhoane slumped onto the only cot in the room and rested his head in his hands. He wasn't sure he could take any more surprises this day.

"The initiates? Why? Why isn't this gift allowed Eleri rulers?"

"I have no idea, nor did I ever question why. I always assumed it was an Eleri custom that only applied to the initiates. Like our ability to choose our mates."

But for the few honored as Verdaine's personal initiates, all other Eleri mated for life. Those studying within the walls of the temple were allowed to choose their lovers and could have more than one in the span of their breeding time. However, for a woman to bed another woman, or a man another man, was forbidden. All coupling must be between a man and a woman to keep the race strong and vital. The laws, as Rhoane likened them, rattled in his brain, as though he were in his father's throne room, hearing the king pass judgment.

Kaleigh handed him the plate of food and pulled a chair close, but kept a discreet distance. "I see this is much for you to absorb. I can leave if you wish."

"Please, stay. The woman you loved, was she an initiate as well?"

Kaleigh took a moment before she answered. When she did, her voice was distant, as if she were once more with her forbidden lover. "We were young then, not much older than you are now, I suppose. All initiates are taught the ways of pleasuring both men and women." At Rhoane's look of surprise, she cautioned, "King Stephan is well aware it goes against his wishes, but it is for practical reasons only. As future practitioners of our faith, it is up to the priestesses to counsel couples how best to conceive children."

Rhoane nodded as his long fingers stroked his chin. "I suppose that makes sense." An image of Carga flashed through his thoughts and he brushed it aside. "Do all initiates participate in the practice?"

"You cannot become a priestess without knowing how to share your body with another. It was a great honor to be skilled in the ways of lovemaking. Some of us would practice on each other, while others preferred to keep their studies to themselves." A wry smile creased her otherwise smooth skin. "Of course, I had to choose one of the latter. She was beautiful in a sad sort of way. She came from humble means, with no family to call her own. I thought if I loved her enough, she would enjoy being at the temple, but her heart was never committed to becoming a priestess."

"The calling is not for everyone." Rhoane sipped a mug of

strong ale to keep his hands occupied. Otherwise, he might be tempted to take Kaleigh's in his own. "My sister is destined to one day become high priestess." The words tasted like straw in his mouth. Was someone, at this very moment, wrapped in her arms? A shudder raced down his spine.

"Do not dwell on her, Rhoane. She knew what was required before Verdaine asked her to become an initiate. We all did."

"In my heart, I know you are right. But she is my sister. I suppose I want to always think of her as being pure, untouched."

"Are any of us pure, Your Highness?"

The question seared through his mind. Her revelations shook his core beliefs, forced him to challenge what he'd always thought to be true. Not more than two bells earlier, he'd killed a man for nothing more than the promise of freedom. Not wanting to dwell on the arena or his sister, Rhoane urged Kaleigh to continue with her story.

"Are you sure?" Doubt creased her features.

He nodded, not really certain of anything anymore.

She eyed the plate of food and waited until he shoveled several bites into his mouth before she took a deep breath.

"One day, I professed my love to her in the only way I knew how. I shared my body with her. She did not fight me, nor did she reciprocate. Stupidly, I took her silence as acceptance and suggested we run away together. She would not have to be one of Verdaine's postulants, I had argued. Was that not what she truly wanted? But I had not really considered her desires at all. I assumed she loved me as much as I loved her. Alas, instead of declaring her love in return, she told the high priestess what I had done. I was stripped of my initiate honor and cast out as sheanna." Kaleigh touched her blonde curls and sighed. "I vowed to never love again. In fact, I spent many seasons finding as many partners as I could and tainting myself with them. I figured if I were forbidden from ever returning to my home-land, I might as well earn my sheanna." A spiteful chuckle escaped her lips. "I nearly died trying to prove they were right to shun me."

"Our laws are harsh. I am sorry." Emotion choked his words and he cleared his throat, keeping his hands firmly around his plate, not trusting himself to offer her comfort. He wanted to touch her too much. To ease the sorrow from her eyes. In them, he saw himself. Saw his own shame.

"How is it you came to be a prisoner here?"

"I told you, I am no prisoner. Amdi saved me. He found me in the foulest brothel of Paderau and brought me to the desert. He once told me he did not want to go to the brothel that night, but his brother forced him. His brother was a nasty man, vulgar and crass—he used women for pleasure, priding himself on how many he could bed in one night. It was dumb luck Amdi found me first. If Deshan had been the first in my room, I am certain I would be as dead as he is."

Something in her tone gave Rhoane pause. "Did you kill him?"

Kaleigh cocked her head and grinned. "Not that night, but the first chance I had, I gutted him like the pig he was. He raped and tortured not just women, but young children, boys and girls, as well. He thought it his right, since he was laird. No one has the right to take another by force." Tears slid down her cheek to drip from her chin. "It took me too many seasons to realize that was what I had done to the girl I thought I loved. I had forced myself on her. It was not right, and I paid for my crime."

"You must have lived out your sheanna. Certainly you can return to the vier?"

"I am sure I could, but Amdi—" Emotion clung to her tone, deepening its resonance. "He loves me, and I am utterly devoted to him."

There was much Rhoane needed to learn, not just about the world, but about himself, it seemed. He had never heard of an Eleri, sheanna or not, choosing to stay away from the vier. Nor had he known being in the presence of a woman could affect him to the point of distraction. He tried to hide his desire, but his glances kept returning to Kaleigh's shapely form. He'd been too protected at the Weirren. Shielded too much from what he would encounter outside the borders of the Narthvier. He was woefully unprepared in all things.

Kaleigh studied him as he waged war within his thoughts. When their eyes met, she nodded as if she'd been eavesdropping. "What made you sheanna?"

Rhoane suppressed a chuckle. He'd been impertinent to ask her—perhaps he owed her the same respect she'd shown by discussing her exile. He sensed in Kaleigh an ally and hoped he wasn't wrong.

"Verdaine." He retrieved the scroll from a hidden pocket of his saddlebags, relief coursing through him it had not been confiscated as well. "She believes I will restore balance to Aelinae by finding the *Darennsai*." He handed the scroll to his clanswoman. "Carga copied the prophecy for me to study. If you would like to read it, I could use your help."

Kaleigh took the scroll from him and scanned the pages. Her eyes grew even larger against her tanned skin. Her breasts rose and fell in quick succession. Rhoane all but heard the tripping of her heart as she paused every so often to fully read a section. When at last she looked up, tears shimmered in her arctic orbs.

"If this is true, then we have much work to do, my prince." She bent to one knee, kissed her thumb before she placed it first to her forehead, then to her heart. "I am beholden to Amdi in all things. I must tell him of this." She paced the space of his tent, a hand to her forehead—the other clutched the scroll.

"What help can your laird be to us?" Rhoane began, but Kaleigh hushed him.

"Amdi means for you to die in the arena. He distrusts the Eleri, sometimes even me." She glanced over her shoulder toward the tent opening. "You will be watched, always. He only let me tend to your wounds as a test, perhaps. He knows I am far more skilled than his healers and wanted to see how I would behave alone with you. Or, it could be he did not want his healers soiled by your presence. I have no idea." She placed a warning hand on his forearm. "You must never look at me like you have here, tonight. You must learn to hide your emotions, especially from yourself. If this prophecy is true, you must meet your chosen one pure. Any dalliance will destroy the bond between the two of you."

Kaleigh talked so fast Rhoane could hardly keep up, but one thing he understood too well. "I know my oath. I will honor it."

"Rhoane, you are a man. There are certain things you have been sheltered from for far too long. Women, among them. You will be tempted many times, but you must not give in to carnal desires. Train your mind as you must train your body. Learn to fight with not just a sword, but your hands, a stick, whatever weapon you can find. Above all else, you can never lose in the arena."

A guard entered the tent and motioned to Kaleigh. "My lady, you have been overlong here. Any longer, and there will be questions."

"I understand." Kaleigh turned to Rhoane, her eyes beseeching. "Do not do anything foolish. Eat. Sleep. Conserve your strength. Amdi will test you in all things. Me, as I said. If you so much as look at me with want, we will both be executed. However, if you can defeat his traps, you will ride away from Ulla stronger for the experience. Trust me."

"Why are you helping me?" He kept his voice low, barely audible.

"Because," mirth marked her words, "the gods know someone has to. You are too hotheaded for your own good. If not for me, you would be dead by morning and that is a travesty none of us can afford. I just need to convince Amdi of this."

After she replaced her headdress, she left in a swirl of dark fabric. The guard glared at Rhoane for several moments until he, too, exited the tent. Kaleigh had taken the scroll with her, and for one mad moment Rhoane started to dash after her, but he halted mid-stride. Let her study the scroll. It might be what would keep him alive one more day.

He eased onto the cot, wincing with every bruise and cut that touched the rough fabric. He stared at the ceiling, cursing himself. His first decision outside the vier might have cost him his life. If he died, what would happen to the Darennsai?

The image of a woman, hair like a cloud on a bright Frost End day, eyes as blue as the deep sea, sprang to his mind. The Darennsai. He was certain of it. But where? Was this in the present, or future? He clung to the image like a frightened child to his mother's hand, not wanting to let go. Afraid of losing the connection. A soft fluttering started in his heart. Something akin to panic blossomed in his chest to spread across his body.

The woman's smile lit up her face and his anxiety lessened. The tent vanished from sight and he stood alone with the woman in a field covered with soft grass and flowers in every shade. She bent to pick several blooms and held them beneath her nose, giggling with the gaiety of a child. The light faded from the sky and she breathed in the scent of the meadow. When he took a breath, he could smell soil and the delicate fragrance of jasmine.

"Who are you?" He longed to reach for her, but feared the dream would end if he did.

"I am your beloved, Rhoane." Behind her, ghost-like, flared a pair of darathi vorsi wings. Silver scales caught the moonlight and she lifted her face to the stars. "Wait for me, my darling. Mi carae." Her fingers stretched between them and she traced along his chin, the feeling as real to him as the terrarae beneath his feet. "Be strong. Remember me." Then she was gone.

Rhoane stared at the fabric of his tent and rubbed his temples, doubting his own sanity. The scent of jasmine clung to the air and he closed his eyes, bringing the woman's face into focus from memory. In one day his entire life had been upended. Everything he once held true was in doubt, but one thing he knew for certain—real or imagined, this woman needed him to keep fighting. For her. For Aelinae. He would wait a thousand lifetimes to hear her laughter. He rolled to his side and there, cupped in his palm, was a single jasmine bud.

CHAPTER FIVE

For near on eight moonturns, Rhoane faced a new opponent in the arena four times a week. Each one more violent than the last. Each one out for his blood. On the nights he wasn't dragged to the fighting ring, he was challenged in other ways. Kaleigh hadn't been wrong when she'd said Amdi would try to break his spirit.

On non-battle nights at sundown, a lovely young woman would bring Rhoane his meal. Dressed in little more than a thin scarf, she would entice him by offering to feed him his dinner. He always refused, yet the woman would stay until he finished eating. Then, the real training began. Each nubile young thing tried various ways to provoke Rhoane's desire. Some would lay their hands upon him, others used dance to seduce him. After the first few visits, Rhoane would cling to the image of the woman with hair of silken stars. He would recall the sound of her voice, the lilt to her tone when she said she was his beloved. Eventually, he learned how to remove himself from the situation. If not bodily, then in mind and function. He became little more than a lifeless figure lying on his cot.

The girls could coo or cuddle all they liked, but he refused to respond. Their attempts to lengthen his manhood failed. Despite their best efforts, they left his tent defeated, disappointed, and, perhaps, disgraced. He didn't care. As long as Amdi tested him, Rhoane vowed to best the laird.

Each night after he battled, Kaleigh would bring his meal and tend to his wounds. He kept his interactions with her polite. The control over his body he learned with Amdi's women served him well in Kaleigh's presence. She never flirted or enticed and kept their meetings as courteous as he, but affection for his clanswoman existed. She was not his Darennsai, but she was his friend and only ally.

Since their first evening, when she'd taken the scroll, she'd not mentioned the prophecy again. Rhoane broached the subject twice, getting a stern shake of her head in reply. He knew the guards stationed just outside his door listened to their conversations and dropped the subject immediately. Still, each time left him frustrated. Kaleigh shared little of her life as Amdi's wife and Rhoane was left to wonder if the chief forbade her from telling Rhoane too much. As if that knowledge might help him somehow gain his freedom sooner.

It wasn't until the ninth cycle of the moon that Rhoane understood Kaleigh's reticence.

Amdi allowed him few liberties in the camp, but on a cloudless morning close to Mid-Summer, Rhoane was not only given access to roam freely, he was told to come with the guard. Intrigued, Rhoane followed the man to a vibrantly painted tent. Swirls of jade, cobalt, and ochre twisted and turned on every inch of the fabric. At the three highest points, black pennants fluttered in the breeze. Two white wavy lines bisected by another two lines stood out against the black. Rhoane contemplated the symbol for a moment before he opened the tent flap and stepped into a cool, dimly lit space. Several men and women waited on cushions set around the edge of the tent. A few drank from tin cups while others rocked steadily back and forth, clutching their arms.

"What is this?" Rhoane asked the guard, but he put a finger to his lips and indicated a smaller room to their right. Through a slight opening of fabric, Rhoane saw figures moving inside. He opened his mouth to speak, but again the guard shushed him. Frustration and his ever-present anger bubbled in his gut. Whatever test Amdi was setting for Rhoane, he'd not let the chief best him. Without asking permission, he tugged aside the flap and entered.

What he saw in the room both horrified and mystified him. On a raised table covered with crimson velvet lay a naked woman, which in itself was startling. To her right, a man, his naked body a gleaming specimen of perfection, guided his manhood into the woman's mouth. She moaned with the effort, and the man's head rolled back. Embarrassed he witnessed the couple's intimate act, Rhoane looked away from him to see Kaleigh positioned between the woman's legs, pleasuring her.

Disgusted, confused, and yet curious, he reeled back, drawing Kaleigh's attention.

Upon seeing him, Kaleigh's eyes narrowed, and a deep scowl creased her forehead. She pushed away from the table and spoke to the couple rapidly in Ullan, most of which Rhoane missed, but her anger came through.

The guard who'd directed Rhoane to the tent—aye, to this very room—chuckled a guttural laugh and left him standing in the doorway, dumbstruck. Amdi had gone too far this time. Forcing Kaleigh to—what? Rhoane wasn't even sure what he'd witnessed.

Kaleigh rose, wiping her mouth on her sleeve, and Rhoane's insides churned. "You should not be here."

"The guard said Amdi wished to show me something." He pointed at the other two. "I can only assume it is this. You making love to another couple." Hostility dripped from every syllable. "Are you his whore as well as prisoner?" The last he spoke in Eleri.

Kaleigh regarded him for a moment. Myriad emotions crossed her features. When she spoke, it was in a tempered tone, as if she, too, held her annoyance in check.

Kaleigh spoke Elennish, slowly, as if to a child. "I am not making love, Rhoane. As I have told you many times, I am not his prisoner. This is how the Ullans heal. The release of energy helps restore health and speed the recovery of wounds." She led him away from the couple and out of the tent before she turned to face him. Anger sizzled beneath her words. "Amdi believes you should come here after each battle. He does not understand why you must be tended by me, even though I do not touch you. He read the scroll and, I believe, secretly worries I am this *Darennsai* the prophecy speaks of."

"But you are not," Rhoane said, his voice flat.

"I know this, and you know this, but Amdi does not. He is jealous. With each win, you gain favor in his court. All I can assume is he wished you to see me healing another so you know I am impure."

At that moment, timed a little too coincidentally to Rhoane's thinking, the laird approached with six of his personal guard close behind. "What are you doing out here, my dove? Are you finished healing my sister?"

Rhoane stifled his surprise. This was still part of the test, he was sure of it. To see if he would reject Kaleigh.

"Not yet. Your intrusion into my work delayed the healing." Kaleigh glared at her lover. "I was making good progress until he showed up." She jerked her thumb toward Rhoane. "Now, I will have to begin anew. Much time has been wasted. If you would like to play games, my laird, please keep the welfare of your people, including your sister, out of them." She turned on her heel and left them gaping after her.

"She has spirit, that woman," Amdi said with pride. "You, as well." He faced Rhoane, who towered over the laird by the span of a man's hand. "I may have misjudged you, First Son."

"I am not like Kaleigh, my lord. I will not heal your people in these tents, nor will I submit to the seductions of the women you thrust at me. I will fight in your arena as long as you see fit to challenge me, but I will not yield. I was born for a higher purpose than to be your plaything, and the sooner you realize this, the better for everyone." At last, Rhoane understood the purpose of his path in Ulla. He was not there to satisfy Amdi's lust for power. He needed to learn control, as Kaleigh had told him so many moonturns earlier. Even seeing her in the healer's tent was part of his learning. Day by day, he'd worked to remain unaffected, to numb his mind and body to the taunts Amdi threw his way, but still he hadn't learned to control his anger.

The stirrings of his ShantiMari warmed Rhoane's blood. He'd not let himself use his power since he left the vier. The image of his mother had been enough to pacify him, but now, he embraced the darkness that swirled within.

"My laird," one of the guards said, warning Amdi of Rhoane's growing need to release his fury, "he calls on the elements."

"You dare call forth your power before me, boy?" Flames lit upon Amdi's palms, and for a brief moment, Rhoane hesitated.

A fight in the arena was one thing, but a ShantiMari battle against the armed Ullan could be suicide. Yet if he backed down now, he suspected Amdi would never let him leave.

"I do. For nine moonturns, you have deprived me of freedom. You have abused my trust, my faith, and my position. I have allowed this. Not because I respect you, but because I hated myself. In those long days of solitude, I found something in me I never expected—hope." Rhoane released his power in a rush. "There is a reason I chose Ulla when I first left the vier. At the time, I did not see the purpose, only my own misery. But you have taught me to be a warrior of the mind and body. Let me be a part of your tribe, so that we might be allies, not enemies." The realization settled upon him with a soft blow. The only person keeping him prisoner in Ulla was himself. He couldn't hate Amdi for trying to protect his people, nor could he resent the man for loving an Eleri woman. His anger slithered from his heart, leaving him feeling lighter, free.

Amdi considered him with cold, calculating eyes. Children ran past, shrieking in excitement after some game they'd been playing. The bleating of sheep drifted over the tents. A lifetime passed in the few moments it took Amdi to make his decision. When his dark eyes softened, Rhoane breathed out a heavy sigh.

"You will fight once more in the arena," Amdi said. "If you win, you may live among us without restrictions."

Ferran's bells, the man was exhausting. Still he abused Rhoane's patience. "I can leave whenever I choose?"

"With the pick of our finest stallions." Amdi's wry smile cracked the tight skin of his burnished face.

"And I can see Kaleigh as often as necessary?"

Amdi's eyes narrowed to dangerous slits.

"She is not my *Darennsai*, Your Majesty. I will not endanger the prophecy by bedding your woman."

"If you survive tonight," the chief said, "you will earn your freedom as my guest, and not a subject."

Rhoane touched his thumb to his heart and gave a heartfelt thanks to the man. He didn't like the ominous edge to Amdi's tone and suspected the night's fight would be far more brutal than he'd experienced thus far, but the promise of freedom was too rich to pass up.

A QUARTER BELL into the fight, Rhoane was seriously thinking death would've been an easier option. His opponent, a titan the likes of which Rhoane suspected had given more than one man nightmares, had entered the arena with all the swagger and confidence of a man who'd already won. He turned slowly in a broad circle, waving to the crowd, enticing them to cheers that rent the evening sky. Rhoane stared dumbly at the man, certain Amdi had planned this from the moment Rhoane arrived at the encampment.

And Rhoane had played right into his deception. Accepted the challenge blindly, without any terms or conditions for the fight. He'd been a fool, and now he was going to die a horrible, painful, inglorious death.

The beast of a man roared, and fresh cheers pierced Rhoane's sensitive hearing. His left eye bled from a vicious punch the man had given him, and his lip was split. His head rang from the blow, and his vision blurred.

Rhoane, Verdaine whispered in his mind, *you can best him. You are young and agile. You are Eleri.*

He drew strength from the fact his goddess had not abandoned him. All those days without anyone for company, and nights spent in battle either with an opponent or one of Amdi's women, had him doubting his sanity and believing the Eleri had forsaken him.

You will one day lead us to a new age, my Surtentse. I will never leave you.

Rhoane steadied himself and eyed his challenger with the cunning of a grierbas stalking his prey. The man was truly enormous. His arm span was twice the width of Rhoane's height, his bicep easily as large Rhoane's girth. But what the man had in brute strength, he lacked in speed and dexterity.

The oaf grinned stupidly, thinking Rhoane weak. He pretended to stagger, all the while surveying his opponent. Around the man's waist, a thick band of leather held a swath of cloth that covered his buttocks and manhood. Other than that, the titan was naked. Weapons adorned the leather belt, including a mace and several small daggers. Rhoane had not been granted the use of weapons, despite the fact he'd won many over the course of his fights in the arena.

Sand danced in a frenzy with each foot the man placed upon

the ground. With every step, his bulk shifted from one leg to another, and Rhoane studied each ripple of muscle as he moved. The crowd roared their approval of the imminent attack, chanting the man's name. "Kragor! Kragor! Kragor!"

Kragor sneered, his smugness fueling Rhoane's ire.

When he was two paces away, Rhoane acted, springing from his stupor to dash toward his opponent. The stunned expression on the man's face would have to be savored another time. Rhoane had mere moments before Kragor would grasp him around the neck and shake the life from him.

As the brute paused, Rhoane used the man's bent leg as a step, grabbed a dagger from his belt, and vaulted up Kragor's body. His opponent resumed his step and slammed his foot hard upon the sand, jostling Rhoane's tentative grip on his shoulder. He almost slipped, but managed to pull himself over the giant. Kragor flailed his hands, trying to reach Rhoane, who used his legs like a vise and clung to the man's back.

Rhoane had planned to slice the man's throat, but his thick muscles and frantically waving arms prevented an opening. A moment of panic swept over Rhoane. The small blade would do nothing to the man if Rhoane stabbed him. Except for one possibility.

Rhoane ducked from being blindsided by a huge fist and strengthened his grip. He grasped the hilt of the giant's dagger with both hands and thrust upward into the base of the brute's skull.

A hush fell over the spectators as Kragor screeched in panicky pain.

The blade sliced upward, through the soft tissue of the man's brain and out through his mouth, slicing his tongue in two. A horrible wailing started in the crowd, women trilling and men shouting. Cobalt blood sprayed over the sand in a wide arc, lengthening as Kragor keeled forward, taking Rhoane with him.

The Eleri loosened his hold a heartbeat before the brute collapsed on the ground and sent dust high into the air.

Rhoane rolled to all fours, coughing against the sand lodged in his throat. His body shook from the rush of adrenaline. He knelt there, gasping and trembling, while the crowd roared. Approval, disapproval—he didn't care. He'd won.

Rhoane took a last shuddering breath and rose to his full height. Chest out, arms at his side, legs planted firmly, he raised his right fist in the air and brandished the bloodied dagger. Sticky blue fluid oozed over his hand, burning his skin. He stood taller, absorbing the pain the other man's vital fluids inflicted. He'd killed for his freedom. He'd not show weakness now.

The tribe clamored loud enough to deafen Rhoane. He stood resolute. He was done fighting for their entertainment.

Amdi approached, his glance wary. Rhoane lowered the dagger and wiped it on his tattered tunic. After a moment's appraisal, Amdi grasped Rhoane's arm at the elbow as his other hand reached around to pat Rhoane on the back. When Rhoane didn't return the gesture, Amdi withdrew. A frown caused deep creases in his forehead and jowls. "Congratulations, boy."

"I am not a boy. And I believe I have won my freedom." Rhoane glanced over his shoulder at the mass of flesh sprawled on the sand. "I require my sword, my clothing, and my belongings, then I will leave your desert."

"You would leave us?" Kaleigh stepped out from Amdi's shadow. No longer clothed in the hooded and veiled garment she usually wore, she stood before her prince in traditional Eleri dress. Rows of scarlet gems dangled from strips of silk, scarcely covering her bare skin. Her skirt rode low on her hips, showing off a golden chain. To Eleri, that single piece of jewelry signified she was taken. Rhoane's gaze went from the gold piece to Kaleigh's face. To see it unadorned and exposed unsettled him.

"Why should I stay?"

"There is much more to learn, First Son."

"I will not fight for him. My battles are done."

"Your battles will never be finished. Not until all facets of the prophecy are fulfilled. If you stay," Kaleigh added in Eleri, "As I promised your first night here, now I will teach you the way of time."

Amdi cut her off with a harsh command to speak in Ullan or Elennish, never Eleri. She lowered her head in acquiescence and spoke to Amdi in Ullan, begging him to allow Rhoane to live among the tribe as a full member, not as a captive combatant. Amdi's nostrils flared. His eyes bore into Kaleigh's, as if a silent argument played out between them.

Rhoane was certain she shared her thoughts with her lover. Something she hadn't done with him. His anger rekindled as he watched the two of them glare at each other, speaking only to grunt a disapproval of something the other had thought. Amdi was going back on his word. Of that Rhoane was certain. But he'd have none of it. If the man refused him his hard-fought freedom, he would take it. By force if necessary.

The sun made a slow dip beyond the mountains to the east, and a chill edged the last heat of the day. It would be dark soon. Time for the night creatures to prowl the skies, looking for prey. Even the guards shifted nervously as they waited for their laird to decide Rhoane's fate.

Except Rhoane had no desire to allow Amdi, or anyone else, to make decisions controlling his destiny. Not even Verdaine, if it came down to it. He would never again be someone's slave. Not Amdi, not another ruler, not even the Darennsai. No one but Rhoane would decide what was best for him.

"My sword," Rhoane said, his tone lethal. "Get it now, or suffer the same fate as him." He didn't have to look at the giant for Amdi to know who he meant.

"You dare threaten me, boy?"

"I am tired of waiting. Either you return my sword to me now, or I will destroy this camp tent by tent until I find it."

"Amdi, please," Kaleigh said. "He satisfied all of your demands. I would like him to stay on as a friend—to train him, and nothing more. But he will not remain unless you act more civil." She leaned in and whispered loud enough for Rhoane to hear, "Someday you will have need of him. I have foreseen this. If you do not honor your word now, you are sentencing all Ullans to death. There is war coming, my laird. Perhaps not in your lifetime, but soon, and this man will be Ulla's salvation. Would you leave your heirs unprotected?"

Amdi's glance swept the thinning crowd. He settled on two sturdy-looking young men. Both tanned, with the burnished skin of the Ullans and dark hair like their father, but with light eyes like their mother. Kaleigh had given Amdi his heirs. It explained why she refused to leave.

"Tomorrow," Amdi said. "You will have your belongings then."

"Why not tonight?"

"Because, First Son, they are hidden in a cave a day's ride from here. Your sword tried to kill anyone who touched it. I had to hide it to be certain no harm came to my people."

A grin broke Rhoane's stern expression. Claidholm Solais would not suffer fools touching him. Rhoane suspected, if he so desired, he could call forth the sword, and it would fly to his outstretched hand. A remarkable idea, but not one he was willing to act upon. Not in front of Amdi and his guards.

"Tomorrow, then." Rhoane bent low at the waist to bow to the laird. "Tonight, I would like to bathe, and then feast with your people."

Amdi barked a laugh and clapped Rhoane on the back. "I think I will like being your friend less than I liked being your laird. At least as my captive, you could not order me around. But for tonight, I will make an exception. I believe we can be mutually beneficial to each other, Prince Rhoane." He clapped his hands, and two women materialized to take Rhoane to the baths.

"Rhoane." Kaleigh lightly touched his arm. *Amdi is still testing you. Be wary. These are his two most skilled concubines.*

Rhoane hid his shock at her speaking in his mind. He hadn't realized the connection was there. All he'd had to do was try. *I am certain Amdi will once more be disappointed. I know now what must be done, and bedding these women is not part of my path. But I thank you for the warning.*

He placed his hand over her fingertips and said loud enough for all to hear, "I look forward to seeing you and your laird at the feast." Internally, he added, *And tomorrow you will teach me to manipulate time.*

CHAPTER SIX

Rhoane stayed in the desert another two and a half seasons. During the day, Kaleigh worked with him, showing him how to bend the Light to slow time and warp the Dark to speed time. At first, they worked in secret despite the close watch of Amdi's guards, meeting under the pretense that Rhoane was showing Kaleigh how better to heal. Eleri skills at healing far surpassed Ullans', and with Rhoane's assistance, Kaleigh became Amdi's best healer.

Although he never entered the healer's tents again, Rhoane often consulted with Kaleigh on difficult ailments, working to find cures to foreign diseases he'd never experienced in the Narthvier. The education was beneficial to everyone. The longer Rhoane lived among the Ullans, the more he came to realize they weren't a warrior race, as he'd first believed. Yes, Amdi demanded all his tribe members learn to fight, but the desert was harsh, and raiders often rode through the camps late at night, trying to steal horses and women.

The encampment moved several times in the space of two seasons—the nine moonturns they'd spent at the base of the mountains was the longest they stayed anywhere. Rhoane suspected it was his captivity causing them to linger overlong in one location, but neither Kaleigh nor Amdi confirmed his suspicions. Yet, shortly after Rhoane's victory over the giant, the entire camp packed up and moved farther to the east, close to the Jansen Strait. The salty tang of the sea had teased Rhoane's heightened senses. He longed to be free of the constant sand and wind, yet he stayed.

His work with Kaleigh and his budding friendship with Amdi kept him with the Ullans. The laird allowed him to sit in on tribal councils, and Rhoane saw a different form of governance than what he knew from the Weirren. Amdi was laird, but his tribal lords held equal power within the tent. Their concerns were heard and addressed by all present. A vote determined the outcome of every decision. Rhoane listened quietly to the meetings, only speaking or contributing to the discussion if asked.

During his two free seasons in the desert, he and Kaleigh pored over the scroll Carga had transcribed. Often, her eldest son would join them. When the scroll revealed no more clues to his path, and Kaleigh could teach him nothing more about folding time, Rhoane knew it was time to leave.

With sadness in his heart, he said farewell to his foster tribesmen, vowing to return again but knowing he might never fulfill the promise. Amdi had presented him with a fine stallion, a dapple grey named Lucitan. Rhoane steered his horse toward the west and Talaith, recalling his sister's prediction the Darennsai would be found in the capital city. For near on a moonturn, he and Luc plodded onward, seeing few riders as they avoided major cities and towns.

After his long sojourn with the Ullans, Rhoane enjoyed the solitude. His days were spent riding, stopping only to fish or trap his dinner. At night, he bunked down under trees, the stars his only source of light. Many times on his journey he sought advice from his goddess, and each time, silence was his answer.

When he finally crested a hill and saw the glittering spires of the Crystal Palace in the distance, he was both relieved and apprehensive. If Carga had seen true, his mate was somewhere in this city. He only had to find her.

AT THE CROSSROAD leading to the palace, Rhoane hesitated. As an Eleri noble, it was his duty to pay respects to the reigning sovereign, but his instincts told him to avoid the palace. Yet the last time he tried to avoid Talaith, he'd ended up in Ulla. Instincts or no, he was not one to shirk his duty. Rhoane turned Luc to the left, keeping the royal pennants in his sights as he traversed the broad avenues. Unlike Ulla, greenery flowered in abundance in the city. Trees rose above the rooftops, and everywhere he looked, blossoms of every shade, shape, and variety spilled from window boxes and garden beds.

The streets were devoid of trash, the cobblestones worn but in good repair. Talaith was a city of wealth, that much was certain. He plucked at his Ullan tunic. Propriety dictated he bathe and change his attire before he presented himself to the empress, but he had neither the resources to find a bathhouse, nor the energy to expend on trivialities. The Eleri garments he'd worn out of the Narthvier were rolled in his saddlebags. The travel-stained Ullan clothing would have to do for now. Once he was established at court, he could see about securing funds. But first, he had to gain entrance to the gigantic shimmering structure that was home to the Lady of Light, Talaith's empress.

The soldier stationed in the guardhouse swept Rhoane with a look of disdain when he requested an audience with the empress, which Rhoane accepted with equanimity. He'd been over three seasons with the Ullans and a moonturn on the road. He most likely looked like a street urchin. Except for Lucitan. No beggar would have a stallion of such fine breeding. Or a sword as magnificent as Claidholm Solais. But a thief might.

A burly man with dark, almost black eyes and deep-brown skin strode toward the gate, his face set in a grimace. Many plaits adorned his head, with curious sounding bells attached at the ends. Rhoane had never met a man who looked like him before. His features and coloring weren't at all like the Ullans, who were more reddish in skin tone, their black hair straight. Rhoane bit his tongue from asking the man from what region of Aelinae did he descend and could they perhaps go there.

In Elennish, the man said, "I understand you wish to see Empress Lliandra." Despite his size, the baritone voice was like velvet. Smooth, with a touch of elegance. This was a man accustomed to his orders being followed. A man probably born to a House of high honor.

Rhoane inclined his head in greeting. "I am Prince Rhoane of the Eleri. I seek an audience with your empress, but first I require a place to freshen up and change my clothing. I am certain your ruler would not appreciate a man too long on the road in her sitting room."

"Sir Baehlon." A pretty lady with auburn curls and eyes of amber strolled past the knight. "Surely you aren't going to keep an Eleri prince waiting? Look at him. He's half-starved and has been too long in the sun. Take him to the east wing. There is an unused room near my father's quarters. He can bathe in privacy and get a decent meal in him before he meets with the empress."

The big man grunted, his look one of consternation and something else, affection perhaps. "And if he is not who he says he is? Will *you* explain to Her Majesty the error of my judgment?"

"Of course." Her smile lit up her entire face and most of the surrounding soldiers' as well. This was a woman respected and admired. Rhoane made a mental note to thank her properly once he'd been cleaned and fed.

A small crowd had grown around them, and the knight fidgeted with the buckle of his scabbard.

"Very well. You there, take this man's horse to the stables. Give him some oats, and make certain he is well tended."

"For shame," the lady scolded, "treating a beast better than our guest."

"Lady Faelara," Baehlon said, "you've already gotten me in enough trouble for one day. Don't tempt my generosity any more than necessary."

Rhoane dismounted and hid a smile. Whatever the relationship between the two, he quite enjoyed watching them volley their words.

"Follow me." The knight turned on his heel and strode away.

Rhoane dipped his head to Lady Faelara. "Thank you."

"Don't make me regret my kindness." Her words hung like steel around his neck.

He jogged to catch up with the knight and fell into step just before they reached a side door that led into the palace. The darkened hallway gave nothing away as to the interior decor, and the stairs they climbed were plain stone. Obviously, the knight had taken him through a servants' corridor, which Rhoane had to admit was a wise choice. The fewer courtiers who saw him in his ragged condition, the better.

They sped down a hallway on the fourth floor of the palace, this one decorated with thick carpets and silk drapes over the windows. Torches lit with ShantiMari brightened the space, and Rhoane counted the doorways they passed. On the eighth one, the knight motioned him inside. The rooms, to his surprise, were opulently decorated. He'd been fairly certain they'd hide him somewhere unobtrusive, but this room was deserving of a high lord, at the least.

"I'll send someone up to help you bathe and dress." The knight moved close to Rhoane, elongating his height until he stood near on a head taller than the Eleri. "I am Baehlon de Monteferron, Champion and Protector to Empress Lliandra. If you so much as look at her wrong, I will kill you." He stared down his nose at Rhoane, unmoving. "Am I understood?"

Rhoane grinned at the man's audacity. "I knew a man once, taller than you, wider than you by far. Perhaps he was a brother? I left him in the Ullan sands bleeding from a head wound." All mirth left his tone and a mask of lethal solemnity slid over his features. "If I wanted to cause your empress harm, she would be dead already."

Baehlon's eyes narrowed to tiny slits. His nostrils flared with his heated breathing. "What's an Eleri prince doing fighting in Ulla?"

"Long story. One I would be happy to tell over a steaming mug of grhom. But if you do not mind, I should like to bathe so I might meet your empress looking somewhat respectable."

Baehlon sniffed with yet another glare and turned to leave. At the door, he said over his shoulder, "If you are who you say you are, be warned. The empress is searching for her next lover, and you're just her type."

"A prince?"

"No." Baehlon faced him. A wide smile broke the tension on his face. "A man."

Rhoane bathed and dressed in his Eleri clothing, doing his best to look like the prince he was. On his way out the door, he caught his reflection and winced. The gaunt face that looked back at him minimally resembled the lad who'd left the Narthvier too full of pride. His naturally pale skin was a shade lighter than Amdi's, his hair a mass of unruly curls with streaks of golden blond. He doubted even his beloved sister would recognize him in this state. Ferran's bells, he hardly recognized himself.

Gone was the sanctimonious sneer he'd once worn as a badge of honor. Reflected in his eyes he saw an intelligence, an understanding of the ways of the world he'd not encountered at home. As he studied the young man who stared back at him, he felt sorry for the lad who had caused his mother's death. The sneer might be gone, but not his anger. Of what he'd witnessed of the world, he wasn't convinced the Fadair were worth what he'd lost. The kindest person he'd met thus far was an Eleri. He recalled the vision he'd had of the woman with platinum hair. She'd called him her beloved. She'd asked him to wait for her. He drew a shaky breath and reminded himself she was worth the fight. The Fadair be damned.

A knock on the door broke his reverie. Waiting in the corridor was a page who led him through hallways and up several flights of stairs, all of which had Rhoane thoroughly confused by the time they reached the huge, ornately decorated rooms of the empress. Without knocking, his escort entered, and he followed. They passed through a small foyer with mirrors on not only the walls, but ceiling as well. Covering the floor, black and white tiles made a bizarre pattern. Not quite checkered, more of cascading Vs with tails flaring off at random intervals. If he stared too long, he became dizzy and disoriented.

Beyond the foyer was a sitting room with floor-to-ceiling windows that overlooked the Summer Seas. He'd never seen the ocean that close before and stared, mesmerized at the expanse of blue. Even in Ulla, the tribe never went as far as the coast, always staying inland, close to mountains, or near the Jansen Strait. The desert people distrusted vast amounts of water. In all his time with them, Rhoane never uncovered the reason why, but here, standing far above the unrelenting waves, he thought he could understand their trepidation. The desert offered safety—the ocean, with its uncertainty and depth, did not.

Rhoane heard the empress before he saw her. A swish of fabric, followed by the scent of roses and lilacs, floated through the air. He turned from the window and swallowed a gasp at the vision before him. Empress Lliandra, dressed in silks of palest blue, her long blonde hair looped and twisted in an ornate style with gems glittering in the fading afternoon light, studied him as surely as he surveyed her. Delicately carved features formed her face. From the gentle arch of her brow, to her straight nose and high cheekbones, down to the bow of her lips, she was perfection. Even her skin—pale, almost white, but with a blush of pink under the surface—was remarkably smooth, like the finest marble.

"I understand you presented yourself as a prince," she said, "and yet you do not bow to me?"

"Forgive me, Your Majesty. I was stunned by your beauty." He bowed low, lower than he had to Amdi, lower even than he did for his own father. "Which I know is no excuse, but the only reason I can give for my poor manners."

"Your Elennish is quite good."

"We are taught the Aelan language in the Narthvier. Father believes it gives us a greater understanding of our neighbors." It wasn't a complete lie. They were taught Elennish at the Weirren, but he'd perfected his grasp of the language in Ulla.

"And your father would be…?"

"King Stephan, Most Favored Son of our goddess, Verdaine. I am Rhoane, First Son of the Eleri."

"So many sons. Surely you Eleri have female children?" Her mocking tone set Rhoane on notice.

A door opened, and Sir Baehlon stepped into the room. "Forgive me, Your Majesty. I was detained on another matter."

The empress waved him off, and he stood to one side, his arms crossed over his chest. "Rhoane was just telling me about all the men in the Narthvier."

Baehlon stood passive, but Rhoane recalled his warning. "We have women as well. My mother, Aislinn, gave birth to four children. Three male, one female. My sister studies with the other novices at Verdaine's Temple."

"I should like to meet your family. Do you think that would be possible?"

"I am not sure. My father is a very private man."

"Is that the reason, or is it because you've been exiled from the forest?"

Rhoane remained unaffected. "My exile has nothing to do with a visit from Your Majesty. That is something you must discuss with the sovereign of the Weirren."

Lliandra strolled to the window until she stood not more than a pace away. She tapped her forefinger along her lips. Every now and again, she bit down on her nail. "I fear I am barren, Prince Rhoane of the Eleri. Tell me, how is it your mother was able to give birth to four children, and I have none? Isn't it true most Eleri have difficulty conceiving even one offspring?"

She moved swiftly. One slender hand went to the front of Rhoane's trousers while the other grasped the back of his neck. He never thought it would happen, but by the grace of his goddess, he thanked Amdi for over three seasons of torturous temptation. It served him well at present. Instead of tensing at her touch, he kept his body soft, his mind alert.

"I need an heir," she hissed. "You come from prolific stock. Perhaps the gods have seen fit to send you here to provide me with a daughter."

Disgusted by the rudeness of not only her touch, but the implication of her words, Rhoane swallowed a curt retort that would surely get him executed. This empress was not one to make an enemy of. He faced her fully, prepared to make an honest objection when they were interrupted by the arrival of a servant, followed by two others.

"His Eminence, the High Priest Brandt kaj Endion, and his daughter, Lady Faelara dal Arran." The servant bowed after his announcement and left the room, but not before his eyes traveled to Rhoane's crotch, a grimace on his lips.

The empress maintained her grasp of Rhoane's nether regions as she gave a quick nod to the newcomers. "Brandt, you've come just in time to meet my new concubine."

An older gentleman sidled into Rhoane's peripheral vision.

"Your Majesty, accosting a noble of the Eleri is a criminal offense." He cleared his throat. "I've heard rumors of Eleri torture, and I'm certain you would find it most unwelcome."

Lliandra's nails cut into the sunburned skin of Rhoane's neck. "I'm sure I would." She smoothed the fabric of his trousers by pressing her palm hard against his flaccid cock. "Perhaps our Eleri guest does not favor the company of women, after all." She stepped away. A look of contempt marred her lovely features. "Just my luck they would send me a eunuch, or perhaps a counterfeit prince."

"I assure you, Empress Lliandra," Rhoane said. "I am neither false, nor do I find you unappealing. I am bound to an oath I took as a lad. My mate has been chosen for me already, and as you might not know, Eleri mate with one person for life."

She eyed his trousers with unabashed longing. "More's the pity for you. Still, we have no proof you are who you claim to be. Until I can determine your business in my kingdom, you will stay confined in a cell."

The high priest cleared his throat. "Again, Your Majesty, I caution patience. There is an easy way to answer your query." He slid a glance at his daughter, who stepped forward and unwrapped Rhoane's sword from a thick wool cloth.

"You went through my belongings?" Irritation seared through Rhoane's patience. He subdued his power and his tone. "Did you find anything else of interest?"

The priest ignored the taunt and beckoned to the empress. "Lliandra, look at the engravings on the blade. They are in an ancient Eleri dialect, and I've yet to decipher the inscription. However, these I can read." He withdrew Carga's scrolls from his robes. "This man is not just an Eleri noble."

"I don't have time for games, Brandt. Tell me who he is."

A flurry of activity toward the foyer caused them all to turn as one. A man's voice could be heard berating someone, and then a gentleman rushed in. His robes flared behind him in a cloud of midnight damask.

"Why is that damned man so insistent on announcing me? You know full well who I am!" The man stopped short when he saw the group. "Ah. That explains it. I was unaware you had company."

"A fact you would've known had you let my seneschal do his job." The empress held out her hands to the man. "Come here, my scoundrel. You've been gone too long and have lost all your courtly manners."

The man embraced Lliandra with the familiarity of a lover. The kiss he gave, although chaste, bespoke later promises, Rhoane was certain.

"Prince Rhoane, if that is who you truly are—and I'm not fully convinced yet—may I introduce you to the foremost mage in all of Aelinae? Alswyth Myrddin. Myrddin has been traveling of late and is just returned to us. What remarkable timing." Her lips grazed the older gentleman's before she indicated her guest. "This young man says he is Prince Rhoane of the Eleri. Brandt was just telling us how his sword proves his identity."

Myrddin bowed to Rhoane, an acceptable depth, but not nearly as low as it should've been for a man of his rank. Rhoane returned the gesture. He'd read about the mage in one of his father's books. The facts of the article escaped him, but he recalled the man had lived longer than anyone, even the Eleri. Four thousand seasons, if memory served.

"A sword, eh? Let us see that." He reached to take the sword from Brandt. A visible spark lit forth from the blade and scalded the man's palm. "It appears your sword doesn't like strangers handling it."

"I could've told you that," Brandt intoned, and Rhoane noticed a wrap around his right hand. *So, he'd tried to handle the sword as well. Served them both right.* "I was just telling Lliandra what this scroll contains."

Myrddin leaned close and scanned the papers. When he finished, he blew out a breath and regarded Rhoane with closer scrutiny. The depths of his blue eyes danced with excitement and merriment. "Not only is this man an Eleri prince, he is the chosen one of the Eirielle."

"What is an Eirielle?" Rhoane asked.

"She is what the Eleri call the *Darennsai*," Myrddin answered. "The Aelans have their own prophecy regarding the future of Aelinae."

Lliandra glanced at Rhoane, a stricken look crossing her features. "It's true? The prophecy?"

Myrddin's face softened, as did his tone. "I'm afraid so, my love. Your days of barrenness are at an end. Now, we just need to find the father of the anomaly."

Myrddin's words sank into Rhoane's consciousness. Understanding dawned at last. The *Darennsai* was not yet born, and, if he understood Myrddin correctly, the empress would be her mother.

Lliandra studied her hand, the one she'd rubbed against Rhoane's trousers, and very slowly wiped it against her skirts, as if trying to remove his taint.

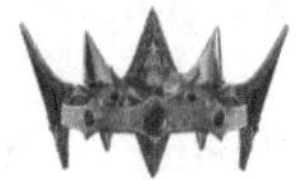

CHAPTER SEVEN

Lady Faelara stormed across her sitting room in an agitated fury. How dare he! How dare her father ask her to do something so improper! She was a lady. Highborn, daughter of the high priest. Both her family names were from respectable Houses. She couldn't be made to act as matchmaker to her empress. Why, it was little more than being a madam. No, she wouldn't. *Couldn't.* He was impossible for even suggesting it.

"Fae, you know I'm right." Brandt settled into a chair and sipped his tea. The tea she'd made for him. *With love!* And *this* was how he repaid her.

"Father, you must be mistaken. The Eleri has only a sword and a scroll. That's not enough to prove anything. And I refuse to even consider your other proposition."

"If you didn't believe he was a prince, then why did you insist he take a room next to mine? And why did you send for me?"

Faelara bit at the nub of her thumbnail and winced when she drew blood. "I was trying to vex Baehlon. I didn't care if the man was a prince or a pauper. It was nothing more than a game to me."

Brandt sipped his tea, and Fae continued to stare out the

window. She knew better than to invite that man into the palace, but Baehlon was being unreasonable and she'd just wanted to show him—what? That he still affected her? Gods, she needed a break from the palace. From Lliandra's frequent tantrums and Baehlon's cluelessness. She inhaled and forced happy thoughts through her chaotic mind. Her gaze was drawn to the bright array of flowers two floors below her window. *Calm.* She needed to be calm in order to deal with her father and his ludicrous suggestion.

The gardens were lovely this time of the season. Not quite summer, but the chill of Frost End had passed. It was her favorite time to be outdoors, hands in the dirt, planting fresh blooms. Perhaps Princess Gwyneira would be available to join her later that afternoon. They could harvest some herbs and practice making potions. Gwyn always enjoyed their little impromptu lessons.

"Are you listening to me?"

Fae turned toward her father. "I was distracted."

"You shouldn't torture Baehlon so much, my darling. He has feelings for you, I can see that, but if you continue with your little games, he will soon lose interest."

A pinch of his brows set off her alarms. "What aren't you telling me?"

"It's probably nothing, but I've heard rumors Lliandra is going to wed him to Lord Askell's daughter."

"Micah? She never said a thing. Why? Lliandra knows I care for Baehlon." Fae swallowed the lump of hurt that lodged in her throat. She'd hinted several times that she would make an excellent match for the knight, and on a few occasions Lliandra had agreed. Faelara knew the answer even before her father spoke.

"For the empress, marriage is done for prestige or promotion. Lord Askell can offer her something I cannot—land and coin." Sadness lingered with the last words.

"Please don't blame yourself, Father. Marrying Baehlon to

someone who can improve her position is perfectly within her rights, but I wish she'd at least told me so I could stop making a fool of myself." Faelara pouted like a child, most unbecoming of a lady, but she didn't care.

For five seasons, she'd been flirting outrageously with the knight. He never spoke of it, but she knew he returned her attraction. Every morning, he would say good day, or bring her wildflowers if he'd been on patrol. Or perhaps she'd imagined he returned her affections, when really he'd been courting Micah. None of it mattered. If the empress decided Baehlon should marry the woman, it was as good as done.

Still, the betrayal stung. Lliandra really should have told her, but the empress did whatever she liked and her subjects rarely had any say in the matter. Far too many times Faelara had witnessed Lliandra's subtle manipulation of courtiers and never spoke up. Now it was she who was left gutted. If anything, she should've expected it. Anger, deep and raw and powerful, cut at the love she once felt for her empress.

"Are you telling me this now to sway my decision?" Fae asked.

Brandt's grin gave him away. He tried to hide it behind the rim of his cup, but she saw through the ruse.

She planted her hands on her slim hips. "You belong in Dal Ferran—a demon you are."

"You would've found out sooner or later. I wanted to spare your feelings before it was too late."

It was far and away much too late. She loved Baehlon and would the rest of her days, whether he returned that love or not. "I suppose this gives me reason to leave court without a scandal." She kept her tone light, her pain suppressed.

"You won't be gone more than a few seasons."

"With a man I've known for less than a moonturn, and only your word to vouch for him." Gods, had the prince really been in Talaith only two fortnights? He'd behaved pleasantly enough, but still. "How can you trust him?" Of everyone at court, Rhoane had spent the most time with Brandt, Myrddin, and Baehlon. If anyone knew him, it would be her father.

Brandt took a drag from his pipe and blew smoke circles before replying. "He survived the Ullan arena for almost a whole season, and even Lliandra couldn't tempt him to her bed. I believe you'll be safe, or I wouldn't suggest this venture." He set aside his pipe and rose to take her hands in his. "He is wary of the world outside the Narthvier and could use a friend. He understands his place in our history and is beholden to all that responsibility entails. But you, my darling daughter, could teach him much. Go with the prince. I'll join you when I can."

"We'll need coin. Prince or no, he arrived without a crown to his name."

"Aye. I'll make certain you have enough to get you to the Summerlands. From there, I'll arrange funds in the various cities you'll visit."

"Does he know? Is he willing to go on a fishing expedition without a boat?"

"I have done a fair amount of preparing him for the idea. Once we explain our true purpose, he'll be more than amenable."

Faelara groaned and shook her head. Sometimes her father was too much of a dreamer. Always studying the stars, his head was permanently in the clouds. She preferred to keep her ambitions closer to the terrarae. Leave the stars to the gods.

In the end, convincing the prince to leave Talaith and the wandering hands of its empress wasn't difficult. Unlike Fae, he had no trouble with traveling Aelinae in search of the perfect man to father Lliandra's child. But Rhoane didn't know the empress like Faelara did. He was unaware of her penchant for beheading any man who didn't give her a child. Nor did he know about the rumors and accusations that the woman liked more than gentle caresses in her bedchamber. Some of the tales Faelara had heard made her blood curdle.

On the surface, Lliandra was as beautiful as they came, but beneath the lovely veneer existed a woman who craved power and wasn't afraid to inflict pain to get what she wanted. She'd never experienced the empress's violence first-hand, and hoped she never would.

Rhoane's enthusiasm for the journey was in complete contrast to Lliandra's reaction when Brandt and Faelara proposed the trip. Despite the Eleri prince's declaration he was bound to another, Lliandra had confided in Faelara on more than one occasion she held out hope he would join her bed and provide her an heir. Rhoane tactfully avoided the empress's advances, but Faelara saw the strain the constant flirting put on the young man. In a way, she felt sorry for him. Lliandra could be most persuasive.

After exhausting themselves arguing with the empress about the importance of the journey, Faelara sought advice from Lliandra's closest advisor, and sometime lover, Myrddin. He generally stayed out of politics, but this was a matter beyond Talaith's borders. If Myrddin couldn't convince Lliandra, Fae didn't think anyone could.

She found him in his tower, tinkering with a box of cogs and wires. The thick spectacles he wore made his deep-blue eyes huge against his face. Stifling a giggle, she examined some of his more unorthodox collectibles: a horse's hoof, complete with bone and fur attached; the beak from a large bird, perhaps a feiche; and nestled among the detritus of his life, a small, leather-bound book with neatly written lines in a language she'd never seen.

"Where do you get this stuff?" She wiped her hands on her skirt. "And whyever don't you believe in having this place cleaned? There's dust here from the last four Ages."

Myrddin scoffed a reply. "Did you come here to besmirch my hygiene? Or was there a purpose to your impromptu visit?"

"I wanted to ask a favor. If you could intervene with the empress on behalf of the Eleri prince, I'm sure he would be grateful. As would most of the eligible bachelors at court."

"Lliandra enjoys the hunt, you know that." He paused in his fiddling and regarded her a little too closely, the spectacles magnifying his inquisitive gaze into something ominous. "You aren't attracted to the handsome youth, are you?"

"Don't be ridiculous. It's just we're supposed to leave on our mission, and Lliandra is preventing us. Whatever her reasoning, summer is upon us, and we shouldn't waste any more time. As it is, I don't see how we can attend the Light Celebrations this Wintertide if we are meant to visit every kingdom looking for suitable donors."

"Donors?" Myrddin's chuckle did little to ease her nerves. "Is that what you call them? Not lovers? Nor companions? Or even paramours?"

"You know what I mean. Don't tease."

"Is this really about the Eleri, or is it that you wish to be away from court when Lliandra makes the announcement regarding Sir Baehlon and Lady Askell?"

Faelara's gut pinched at the mention of the couple. "It's true I don't wish to be a part of their happiness, but I am here solely for the benefit of our empress. She must produce an heir. If she doesn't have a female child within the next ten seasons, the crown will pass to Gwyneira. I'm sure the princess will make a fine empress, but never in the history of Aelinae has one sister had to give up the throne for another. I'm afraid of what might happen should that come to pass."

Myrddin bent his head to his box of springs and gadgets. "Lliandra's crown is safe, for now. But you make a valid point. I'll speak with her tonight. In fact," he glanced up, his eyes luminous, like the vast night sky, "I'll insist I travel with you and the Eleri. If her reservations are tied in any way to you and the prince having an improper dalliance while on your journey, my presence should alleviate that fear."

"You would do that? Oh, thank you, Myrddin." She flung her arms around his neck and kissed his cheek. "Having you along will make the search that much easier. I confess, finding a suitable donor for the empress does have me a bit vexed. Where to look? What are the qualifications? Will he even be interested?"

"My dear, you worry too much about these things. There isn't a man alive who would decline the chance to bed Lliandra. She is the most powerful woman in all seven kingdoms. The question you should be asking yourself is, 'Who will provide the empress with the Eirielle?' That's the only qualification we need concern ourselves with."

Myrddin ignored the fact the Eleri had not only denied Lliandra, but had publicly stated he would remain untouched until his true mate was found. Lliandra had been in a snit all that day, and Faelara had feared for the prince's life. The man might have survived Ulla's arena, but life at Lliandra's court required a set of skills the Eleri obviously lacked. Fae was determined to keep Rhoane alive long enough to find this elusive donor of Lliandra's heir. With the donor in her bed, and the Eirielle a reality, Lliandra's power would weaken.

Not that Faelara wished her empress harm, but a lesson in humility might be for the best. The woman thought she could play with people's emotions, as if she owned them. They were her subjects, not her source of entertainment. Faelara pressed a clammy palm against her racing heart. Her thoughts were treasonous and could never be spoken aloud. Yet she craved to see Lliandra on her knees, begging for mercy. The woman had stolen something precious from Faelara. It wasn't right she get away with it.

"Where do we look for such a man?" Her voice came out no more than a whisper.

"I have a feeling he will find us." Myrddin took her hand in his. "The trick will be in knowing when he does."

Three days later, with Lliandra's blessing, the small group left Talaith's harbor aboard a fine vessel. Their goodbyes had been brief, their saddlebags packed with only essentials. Faelara glanced at the crowd gathered along the docks, waving farewell to the sailors who manned the ship. Baehlon stood off to the side, his face like a storm about to break. She committed every detail about him to memory. The stance of his feet, planted to the dock, the deep mahogany of his skin, the way his muscles flexed as he crossed and uncrossed his arms. All of it, she stored away in her heart.

Before he could turn away, she met his dark eyes, willing all the love she'd ever had for him into that final stare. For a heartbeat, she thought she saw something—longing perhaps, or remorse? She couldn't say. Then he turned, his black braids swishing with the movement. She was too far to hear the delicate bells he wore in each braid and yearned for the sound. But she knew Baehlon was truly lost to her. He'd accepted the empress's command to marry Micah without so much as an argument. It was his duty, he'd said. He was the Lady of Light's Champion and Protector—how could he say no?

Faelara hadn't cried in front of him. Instead, she had steeled herself against the anguish his actions caused. She knew he loved her, but he loved their empress more.

She would never forgive him.

CHAPTER EIGHT

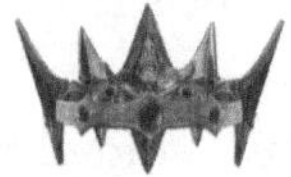

Rhoane gazed at the strangers' faces without seeing them. They'd come to say farewell to loved ones, but he had no one in the crowd who waved to him. Off to the side, he saw the knight he'd first met at the gates of the palace, Sir Baehlon. His expression spoke of suppressed rage, and Rhoane wondered at the cause. The man's eyes were fixed on a spot to Rhoane's left.

On Faelara. Her face was a study in restraint. She was being brave, but beneath her calm demeanor, he sensed a fury equal to Baehlon's.

"Fine day for a voyage." Myrddin clapped Rhoane on the shoulder and chuckled genially as he strode away. He bent to say a few words to Faelara, who nodded in answer, her glare never leaving the dock, and then the mage ambled off.

Indecision stayed Rhoane's tongue. In the moonturn he'd been at court, her father had befriended him and he felt a sense of loyalty to the high priest, but he wasn't sure Faelara would welcome his sympathy. Baehlon turned away from the ship and disappeared in the crowd. Rhoane glanced once more at Brandt's daughter and placed a reassuring hand on her shoulder. He'd been mistaken. Fury whirled beneath his touch, yes, but also there existed heartbreak. Like a clock chiming, and cogs fitting into place, he understood. Faelara loved Baehlon, and if he had to guess, the knight loved her as well. He gave a slight squeeze and her eyes met his. Agony was writ in her features and unshed tears shimmered beneath dark lashes.

A slash of guilt cut at him. "I am sorry if I am the cause of your sadness."

Faelara's sullen chuckle did little to ease his mind. "You are my salvation, Prince Rhoane. Never my sadness." She placed a hand over his and smiled. "But thank you."

The ship lurched, and Rhoane's stomach flipped several times. He left the railing to find a comfortable place to endure the horrors of the trip. Baehlon had said sailing was like riding a horse, but this was nothing like being on horseback. The sway of decking beneath one's feet, the constant shifting of water tossing the ship, was a special kind of torture.

He climbed down the steep ladder that led to where they kept the horses below decks. Lucitan nickered when he approached, a wild look in his eyes.

"Easy, boy. They tell me this will get easier." He petted Luc's muzzle and neck, smoothing out his fine grey coat. "You are a desert creature and I from the forest. This is unnatural for both of us. But we shall overcome, yes?"

He spent a good portion of the day with the livestock, grooming Luc and the other horses. Their coats shone in the dim light of his drossfire globes. A lad arrived some time later to feed the beasts, and Rhoane assisted. Wordlessly, they tossed flakes of hay to the horses, breakfast scraps to the pigs and goats.

When they'd finished, the lad thanked Rhoane. "You best be gettin' upstairs. The cap'n will get sure sore if you aren't at the table when supper's ready."

On his way to the main cabin, Rhoane heard a scuffle down a darkened hallway, followed by the muffled cry of a woman. He turned toward the sound, his hand reaching for his sword, but it was locked in a chest in his room. Captain's orders—no weapons allowed on his ship.

He crept down the corridor careful to not make a sound. One hand traced along the wall, the other held in front of him. Even with enhanced Eleri sight, the corridor was too narrow and too dark to make out a slipped board or sudden turn. A loud cry, followed by a slap, had him shrugging off his concern for stealth and running blindly in the dark. A glowing orb filled with his ShantiMari sprang forth and bobbed before him, lighting a pace or two of the cramped space. He turned a corner, and there, a man tangled with a woman. Light from a nearby cabin lit his profile, but Rhoane didn't recognize him. The woman, however, he did.

"Faelara!" he called, and the man froze in his attack. He turned to face Rhoane, his cheeks reddened with scratches, his throat dripping blood. She'd fought the man with the bravery of an arena combatant. "Get off her, you trollop's cur."

Rhoane grasped the man's shirt and tore him from Faelara. His fist smashed into the attacker's nose, and blood poured over his lips. A knee connected with Rhoane's privates, which knocked him backward and gave the man enough space to run off in the opposite direction.

Rhoane wheezed a moment, his head dizzy, his body flooded with pain. Faelara gasped as well, her hands clinging to her torn gown. Rhoane pushed aside his discomfort and rose to face her. "Are you hurt?" He scanned her face and body, noting bruises around her neck, scratches to her chest and arms.

"Nothing a bit of salve and wine won't cure."

"He did not—?"

"No, thanks to you. Had you been but a few minutes later, I'm afraid he might've succeeded."

Rhoane glared at the darkened hallway. "What are you doing here, alone?"

"I came to fetch a shawl. I have no idea where he came from.

One moment, I'm unlocking my cabin—the next, he was on me like a starved crellion and I a tender doe."

"Get changed, and I will escort you to dinner. After we dine, I will find this man and make certain he does not bother you again."

"Thank you, Rhoane, but I'm fine. Really." Her rapid pulse beating beneath the fragile skin of her neck and the slightly acrid smell of perspiration gave away the lie.

"We must tell the captain."

"Please don't. He didn't want to take us on his ship. He said women were bad luck, and if you tell him one of his crew attacked me, he'll believe I seduced the young man. He's of the old way and thinks women belong on shore servicing their husbands, not out adventuring."

"He is a fool," Rhoane grumbled.

"I won't argue that. Wait here. I'll be but a moment."

She returned wearing a different gown with a high neckline, a shawl wrapped tightly around her shoulders. None of the scratches or bruises could be seen. By the time they found the main cabin and their seats at the table, soup had already been served. The captain gave Rhoane a saucy wink but reserved his contempt for Faelara. Throughout the meal, he made lewd comments about a woman being aboard his ship and how best they could make use of her services.

With each repulsive comment, Myrddin met Rhoane's glare and gave a slight shake of his head. After dinner, the men were invited to join the captain in his private quarters to dice and play cards. Since Faelara was not allowed to accompany them, Rhoane chose to stay with her above deck.

On their way out of the cabin, Rhoane pulled Myrddin to the side. "Faelara is not safe aboard this ship. She was attacked, and only by the grace of our gods did I find her before the cur took her maidenhead. Either you or I must guard her at all times."

Myrddin's blue eyes held none of the mirth so often found

within. "I was afraid of something like this happening. Leave it to me. I'll put a ward on her. If someone so much as touches her, you and I will know." He took Faelara by the elbow and led her up the stairs to the main deck. Rhoane followed.

They argued briefly before Faelara gave her acceptance. The hair on Rhoane's forearms rose when Myrddin placed the ward. Myrddin's ShantiMari was ancient. Much older than any Eleri's. It prickled against Rhoane's skin and scratched against his own power. Myrddin gave them both a command to be alert and cautious, then left to join the captain and his men.

Tears glittered in Faelara's eyes when she finally turned to face Rhoane. "How could you tell him? He's my father's closest friend. Once he learns of the attack, he'll insist I come home."

The ship pitched slightly, and Rhoane gripped the railing like a man clinging to the side of a cliff. "Be angry if you will, but I cannot live with myself if you are harmed."

The ship tilted again, and his stomach churned violently.

"You are positively green, Rhoane. Have you never sailed before?"

"Never. Nor had I seen the ocean before reaching Talaith."

"How remarkable. I guess I never thought someone might live their whole life and never see the seas. May I?" She reached toward his forehead and he blanched. "And now you're white as a snowdrop. Honestly, are you always this fidgety around women?" Her hand hovered close to his face. "I only want to ease your seasickness. Nothing more." She snorted in an unlady-like manner. "Trust me, I'm not looking for a beau at the moment. If ever." He gave a quick nod toward her fingers and she lightly touched his cool skin. Instantly, warmth spread through him, settling his stomach and calming his anxious pulse.

Her ShantiMari was infused with caring, like his mother's had been. "Thank you, Lady Faelara." He took a half-step back, to end their connection.

Her eyes narrowed and she tapped a finger to her lips. "You don't trust women, do you?"

"Some yes. Most no."

Her spontaneous laughter bounced across the empty deck. "I appreciate your honesty. I meant what I said. I do not want a lover, a husband, or a tryst. I know you are committed to the Eirielle and I will respect that. I do hope someday you will trust me." She took his arm and skillfully changed the subject. "I suppose this trip is new for both of us. I've been aboard ships going from Talaith to Paderau, but never on the ocean. It helps if you keep your knees flexible to sway with the rocking."

"I will endeavor to remember that. Thank you." He squeezed her fingers where they rested upon his sleeve. Nothing more needed to be said. He relaxed, knowing he and Faelara could be friends.

"Tell me, was Ulla as horrifying as one is led to believe? Do they truly castrate anyone who loses a battle in their arena?"

Rhoane suppressed a laugh. "Not that I witnessed, and I have to say, I am glad they do not!"

As if realizing the import of her question, her eyes grew wide. "I'm sorry, Your Highness. I forgot you did battle."

"I wish I could forget those battles." Rhoane's voice dropped with the memories of too many nights entertaining Amdi, too many opponents' deaths. "I did not always win, and there were many nights I did not know if I would survive, but the Ullan chief demanded I fight for my freedom."

"He held you captive?"

"More or less. I am sure I could have fought my way out, but there was no honor in that path. I chose to stay as a penance, perhaps. Or a way to learning. I am not sure. It does not matter now because I am stronger for the trials I encountered. Certainly, you have had strife in your life as well?"

Her laughter floated over the dark water. "What a horrible predicament you have created for me. If I say yes, you will laugh at the trivialness of my strife, and if I say no, you will call me false."

"I would never laugh at the suffering of others, no matter how it differs from my own. Pain does not have limitations."

She squeezed his arm. "No, it doesn't. Shall I entertain you with tales of my childhood, and what it's like to be raised by a man who some consider quite strange?"

"Your father did not strike me as anyone other than a curious being who wished to explore the many intricacies of this thing we call life."

"You are kind, Prince Rhoane. Yes, my father is curious, and quite intelligent. I often assist him with his experiments. Do you know, he crafted a machine for studying the stars? We got the idea from Myrddin's magnifying spectacles, actually. My father could spend bell upon bell studying the stars, always asking what was beyond the glittering swaths of sky."

Rhoane stared at the twinkling lights. It had never occurred to him anything might live beyond them, believing everything he knew and loved lived among the trees of the Narthvier. He'd been naïve then, an innocent boy, but no longer. If there were ships that could sail upon the sea, and giants who fought because their laird ordered it, what else was there to discover? The stars gave no answers, unfortunately. They did, however, create the possibility of many more questions.

Faelara spun tale after tale of her father and his inventions. It was several bells later that Rhoane shared with Faelara his trials with the Ullans. He told her of his battles in the arena, and with Amdi's concubines. While he accepted the Ullans were skilled healers, he refrained from telling her details about the Ullan's unique way of healing. He wasn't sure why, but divulging that to the refined lady felt like a betrayal to Kaleigh. He did not share why he left the Narthvier, nor did Faelara ask. Instead, she regaled him with tales of her childhood. Her mother had died when she was very young, and Brandt raised her alone. With each new story, he sensed the loss of her mother even more. Rhoane understood her grief all too well.

When the moon was no longer visible and Faelara stopped trying to hide her yawns, Rhoane escorted her to her cabin, stopping first at his own. He searched through his belongings until he found two palm-sized daggers. Not quite throwing knives, but deadly enough.

"I want you to keep these with you at all times. Tomorrow, I will show you how to use them. We will also train with a sword in hand-to-hand combat. If you insist on accompanying me, these are my terms."

Faelara held the daggers on her open palms. A slight shake gave away her nerves. "I will do as you ask, but you must also teach me your ways of healing. Not just Eleri. I wish to know all there is about Ullan healers, as well. I have a feeling being a skilled healer will come in handy around you."

Rhoane suppressed a grimace. "Of the former, I will. Of the latter, I am afraid I did not actively participate in Ullan healing."

"Whyever not? I'm sure they could've used someone with your skill." At his hesitation to reply, she prodded, "What aren't you telling me? Please, I thought we were friends. Whatever you say will stay with me, I promise."

Trapped in his tiny cabin, with no escape except the door where Faelara stood, his unease curled around them like a vine full of thorns. Faelara stood watching him, her eyes luminous in the dim light. In their depths he saw curiosity, perhaps the same spirit that moved her father to create a looking glass to the stars. In those depths he was lost. Not like a love sick lad, but lost to denying her any sort of information that could educate and enlighten. In her, he saw not a highborn lady, but a young woman desperate to better herself and, ultimately, her world.

He drew a shaky breath and said in a near whisper, "Ullans use coupling to heal. They believe it releases power through channels not otherwise accessible."

"Oh." A furious blush darkened her pale cheeks. "That's too bad for both of us." She laughed at his stricken look. "I'm jesting with you, Rhoane. I know you're promised to another, and I would never do anything to compromise your oath. Gods truth, with all the women Amdi threw at you, you'd think by now you'd understand women much better." She tapped a long nail to her lips. "It does make me think you should learn to at least flirt. You're much too serious and stiff around women. Loosen up a little. Flirting is a great way to get information. Trust me." Her devilish grin contrasted beautifully with her youthful innocence.

Rhoane definitely didn't like where the conversation was leading. "Since there is no need to flirt here, we will focus on weapons training."

"That's where you're wrong, Prince Rhoane. Flirting is not just limited to the opposite gender. But there is plenty of time to teach you the finer art of seduction." She tried to stifle a yawn, but instead made a sound loud enough to wake a vorlock from slumber. "Pardons, please! I'm afraid you've exhausted me. If you will?" She stepped into the cramped hallway, and Rhoane followed to her cabin.

Once she was safely inside, he prowled the quiet ship in search of the man who had attacked his new friend. He found the wretch hiding in the storage hull, curled against a barrel of ale. He knelt in front of the sleeping man for a long time, debating his next move. If he killed him, the captain would think the ship haunted due to Faelara's presence. Plus, killing him would be a mercy.

After securing the man's wrists and ankles to make certain should he wake, he couldn't leave, Rhoane set out for the captain's quarters. The sun would be up soon, and he didn't have time to waste.

When the morning watch arrived on deck early the next morning, they found a very inebriated deckhand, naked except for the captain's coat, wrapped around a snoring sow.

THAT NIGHT AFTER DINNER, Rhoane led Faelara to the captain's sitting room, where the other men were already engaged in their entertainments. When the pair entered, the captain bellowed for Faelara to leave, but Rhoane held firm. He would not allow the man to punish her simply because she was a woman. He'd seen plenty of females who could outwit, outmaneuver, and outwork men. Playing cards should be no different.

Faelara settled into a seat opposite Myrddin, her nervousness carefully hidden beneath a friendly exterior. Rhoane watched her as he and the others were dealt a hand of cards. A slight tremble to her fingertips, repeated biting of her lower lip, and an octave-higher speech were the only signs of her discomfort. She'd argued when he'd first proposed the scheme, but in the end, he'd won by stating if she didn't take a stand, the captain would continue to view women as little more than harlots bred for men's carnal desires. That won the argument without another word.

A short time after their arrival, the atmosphere in the room relaxed. The more wine was poured, the looser the men's tongues became. They joked about the deckhand and his companion. Some thought his punishment of serving out the remainder of their journey in the livestock holds was too lenient. These men had demanded the deckhand be castrated and tossed overboard for King Baldev to devour.

Others in the room thought the punishment fair but cautioned against putting such a man in charge of the livestock. These quips got the most laughs out of the sailors. Each time a comment was tossed forth, Faelara's lips would loosen the tiniest bit, until she, too, laughed at the ridiculous scenarios the men created. She was soon bantering with them as if she'd grown up aboard the ship. By the end of the evening, she'd quite charmed each and every one. Rhoane kept his surprise in check, but secretly studied the way she expertly wrapped their hearts around hers. If this was flirting, as she'd called it, he was indeed impressed. He realized he'd need more than a few lessons in the skill.

"Tell me, Captain, how is it such a handsome man as yourself, who I'm sure has no small amount of ladies vying for your attention, has chosen such an isolated life?" Faelara toyed with her cards, debating which to lay on the table. "Although, I do suppose the sea, as glorious as she is, deserves no less than a man like you to rule her."

The captain straightened in his chair, his chest puffed slightly. "I admit, the sea is as welcoming as any lover, and often just as feisty. Why choose this life? Ohlin's truth, I didn't. It chose me. From the time I could toddle, all I ever wanted was to be on the water."

"Well," Faelara lowered her lashes with a sly smile, "the mainland is sorry for the loss." Her gaze swept the others. "For so many losses." A slight stain brightened her cheeks. "For surely such brave lads as you would make equally fine husbands and fathers. I can almost imagine the sons and daughters you'd raise. Independent, with strong hearts and adventuring souls. Aye, I can tell you are men of honor and would never mistreat women."

The men protested her praise, but it wasn't with much force. They agreed to a man they valued women. In fact, some offered, they'd thought of leaving sea life for a girl back home. Rhoane met Myrddin's inquisitive gaze and nodded. With those few words, Faelara secured her safety on the ship. None of them would dare prove her wrong.

After five more nights of gaming and studying the way not only Faelara, but the men flirted, Rhoane tired of the entertainments and ventured to the upper deck for fresh air. Despite his best efforts, he couldn't grasp the subtle art of words in the same way Faelara had. He determined his would be a life devoid of flirtatious mastery.

It didn't take long for Rhoane to regret leaving the relative comfort of the captain's quarters. The sea was especially ornery this night, tilting the ship from one side to the other until his insides wished to be outside. He gripped the railing, willing his gut to settle.

"Perhaps if you did not fight it, you would feel better?"

Rhoane swung around to see who had joined him, and the wine he'd drunk swirled dangerously close to making an exit.

"Rock with the ship. Feel the waves beneath you." Faelara stood a few paces from where he clung to the railing. "Relax your knees. Bend into the ship. Become one with the sea."

Rhoane shook out his legs, lessening the tension in them, and tried what she suggested. Rocking with the ship helped somewhat, but his stomach continued to roil.

The ship pitched to the right, and he slammed against the rigging. "How much longer must we suffer on this damned vessel? I do not enjoy storms on land, much less so at sea."

"A few more days, I would imagine. Although, if you keep insulting the sea king, he might prolong your misery."

"You believe in fables, Faelara? I would not have thought it."

Faelara leaned against the rail, her face upturned to the clouds. A spray of seawater dappled her skin, but she made no move to wipe it away. "I believe in all things, Prince Rhoane. Who is to say a fable is of any less value than a prophecy? Often, the two are closely related, but only those curious enough will uncover their meaning."

Rhoane scoffed. He'd heard enough about prophecies in his short life to know they were nothing like children's stories. "A fable is nothing more than empty words strung together to entertain the weak-minded."

The wind picked up and whipped their hair around their faces in a tempest. Faelara let her curls unfurl from their pins and spread her arms wide. "The problem with thinking you know everything is that someday you'll discover you know nothing." She smiled sweetly at him. Her pale skin shimmered in the moonlight as if she were graced with Glamour. "My father loves to remind me of this right before he proves I'm wrong."

"And are you trying to prove me wrong?"

She turned to face him, her back to the ocean. "Whatever could you be wrong about, Prince Rhoane?"

"You mock me."

"No, I just think you've lived a very isolated, one-sided life." She tilted her face toward the stars, then gazed at the water. "Do you swim, Your Highness?"

He shifted his weight with a violent rock of the ship. "If you consider sitting in a tub of hot water swimming, then I excel at it."

Her laughter burst from her, as surprising as thunder on a summer's day. "Forgive me. I didn't expect humor from you."

"I imagine there are all kinds of things you would not expect from me." He did his best to cast a flirtatious tone to his words. They felt stiff and uncomfortable on his tongue.

"You have no idea what I can imagine."

Rhoane swallowed the surge of concern that came with interacting too closely with a woman. "And you forget I have lived with the Ullans. My imagination is perhaps more educated than yours." This time the banter came easier, more playful.

"Very good, Rhoane. I would caution, however, to be aware of never going too far. The person you are flirting with still has feelings and might expect you to act upon your words. Innocent flirting or no, they might believe your intentions are true."

"I admit, that was strange for me. I had, not more than a bell past, decided I would fail terribly at flirting. Perhaps in time I will achieve better command of the process. I will remember your words of caution." The ship swayed and he grunted. "I admit I am envious of your skill with words as much as I am with your ease at sea."

"I feel at home in the water, sometimes more than on land. Did you know the Menurrans hold competitions each summer to see who is the best swimmer? I was thinking I might enter if we're there for the celebrations."

Rhoane suppressed a shudder. Water deeper than his ankles had always frightened him. He could recall with excruciating detail the sensations of dread that crisscrossed his body each time he had to witness a purification. Knowing that he, too, would someday be submerged in Lan Gyllarelle gave him no comfort. Where the fear of water came from, he had no idea. He just knew he and any body of water were not allies.

The wind grew stronger, and lightning flashed through the dark clouds. Crew members darted here and there to tighten rigging and prepare the ship for a storm. Rhoane avoided looking at the ocean. The white caps atop turbulent waves were not the last things he wished to see before he bedded down to what promised to be a fitful night's sleep.

"We should be inside." He took Faelara's elbow and guided her through the melee of sailors. Once they were at the door to her cabin, he released his hold. She thanked him and turned to open the door, then paused.

"Rhoane?" She waited for him to face her. "Do you truly believe we are only meant to have one mate?"

"Most Aelans do not share the Eleri custom of mating for life. I would not expect you to understand, but yes, I do think there is only one person we are meant to share ourselves with."

Her face fell, and he tucked a stray curl behind her ear, cupping her cheek with his palm as he did so. The intimate gesture surprised both of them. Her skin was warm despite the chilled air, and he wondered at the meaning behind her question.

"More flirting?"

"Genuine concern. I did not mean to upset you." He searched for words to comfort her. "You are not bound by Eleri customs and are free to choose your mate. If there is a man you desire, what is stopping you from pursuing him?"

Her wry smile did not lift his spirits. Instead, he felt his words had made the situation worse.

"You're very kind to say so, but I'm afraid that's impossible. You see, the man I love is, most likely, marrying another woman at this moment." She opened the cabin door and turned away from him. "You are not the only one locked into a life over which you have little control."

Her words hovered around him long after she'd closed the door. He didn't know Faelara well enough to know whom she meant, but guessed it was Sir Baehlon. He recalled her glare at the man on the dock before leaving Talaith's harbor. If in fact Baehlon had scorned her, he was a fool. Faelara was a woman worth fighting for, of that Rhoane was certain.

He ambled to his own cabin, rocking with the ship and hating the queasiness in his gut. It was true—he envied Faelara's ease on water, her ability to adapt to sea travel, and her enjoyment of the ocean. She was a remarkable woman, and for a brief moment, he allowed himself to imagine what it would be like if he could choose his mate. Would Faelara be his equal in everything? Or even Kaleigh? He scanned his memories of the Eleri women he knew, and none of them enticed him.

Even with Kaleigh's gentle nature and Faelara's intellect, they were not meant for him. His thoughts lingered on Faelara, most likely reclining on her bunk, yearning for her lost love. That's what Rhoane had done for much of his childhood—yearned for a future he could not control. He sat on his own cot and ran his hands through his short hair, cursing the oath he'd made. It changed nothing, he knew, but after a lifetime of holding onto his own truths, he didn't know how to rewrite the story. How to accept what was expected of him could be good, for not only him, but Aelinae.

The ship rocked to one side and he firmly set his mind upon the woman with silver hair who'd come to him once, long ago.

Time had not faded his memory and she filled his dreams until the next morning when he woke to calm seas and clear skies.

Their journey to find his Darennsai's father did not seem strange to him. Yet, if someone else were to tell him they were on a similar quest, he'd think them daft. Whoever sired the Darennsai, Rhoane suspected it would be someone the gods found worthy. Whether that be a ruler or a beggar, he couldn't say. Faelara steadfastly believed the father must come from noble blood, but Rhoane wasn't as certain. Although, the brief time he'd spent at the Crystal Palace had convinced him Lliandra would settle for nothing less than her equal. Which should make their search a quick one. But Aelinae was vast, and time finite. None of the prophecies said when the Darennsai would be born. For all Rhoane knew, Lliandra wouldn't be the mother of the Darennsai. Ferran's bells, for all he knew, the prophecies were nothing more than children's stories. Truth was, they wouldn't know anything until the child was born.

Rhoane rose from his cot and silently made his way to the upper deck, where he gazed out over the dark ocean. The sun was just breaching the horizon and he chuckled at Faelara's belief in King Baldev, ruler of a great sea kingdom whose inhabitants lived beneath the waves. Fairytales and poppycock.

CHAPTER NINE

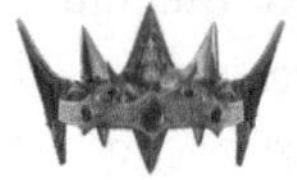

They docked with no fanfare, nothing to indicate the ship carried three prominent persons. Once the gangplank was lowered, the captain ordered their horses unloaded first. His gruff expression and harsher than usual commands alerted Rhoane's group that he was in no mood to be trifled with. Goodbyes were short, if given at all. The trio was equally as eager to be on solid ground. Faelara, having exhausted all of her compliments on the crew during the voyage, skipped down the gangway first, followed closely by Rhoane, then Myrddin. The mage looked as if he'd hardly slept in several days, with dark moons resting beneath his eyes.

They rode through the streets of the Summerlands capital in silence. Rhoane and Faelara discreetly admired the well-trimmed houses and shops they passed, while Myrddin slunk into his saddle, as if dozing. His hood covered much of his face, and every so often a sleepy snort issued from the depths of the fabric.

Menurra was nothing like anywhere he'd been. The broad avenues were flanked by coral colored archways and colonnades. Tall buildings of the same shade rose from the overhangs three, sometimes four stories high. Windows with arches ending in delicate points reminded Rhoane of Eleri's ears. A hand went unconsciously to his own. How intriguing that a culture far from the Narthvier could remind him of home.

Mosaics covered entire squares, their colorful tiles dirty from the many hooves trampling across them. The people of Menurra wore either dun colored tunics and wide legged trousers, or filmy tops and skirts that competed in vibrancy with one another. Their copper skin and black hair added to their beauty, contrasting perfectly with the pale buildings and jewel toned clothing. On several of the women, he spied ropes of golden chain dangling from midriff baring blouses and circling their waists. The people did not appear in a hurry, nor did many of them grimace beneath the sun's relentless heat. In fact, most of those he passed smiled to the trio, their faces a mixture of curiosity and welcoming. His unease from the ship sloughed away with each step Lucitan took up the cobbled street.

At the palace gates, Myrddin roused himself and asked whether the king and queen would accept an audience with an old friend. Rhoane exchanged a glance with Faelara. Her furrowed brow and narrowed eyes answered his unspoken question. The empress had promised to send messages to each of their respective stops along the route; certainly, the king and queen would be expecting the group. Yet Myrddin hadn't mentioned their names, or their mission.

They followed a young groom to the stables and left their horses in his care. Several pages retrieved their meager possessions and indicated the visitors should enter the palace through the main doorway before scampering off in the opposite direction.

Another page escorted them through the colorful hallways decorated with mosaic tiles that depicted scenes from the sea. One in particular of Menurra's harbor with dozens of ships ready to sail into the distance captured Rhoane's attention. Almost hidden between two dolphins, the artist had skillfully inserted a mermaid into the scene. A broad smile lit up her face. For a moment, he thought he could hear her laughter.

"Rhoane, did you hear me?" Faelara touched his sleeve, and he shook his head.

"I was distracted. I am sorry."

Her smile was not nearly as joyful as the mermaid's. "I said, the king and queen will see us now."

He glanced at the mural again and caught the splash of mermaid tail as she swam away. The tiles must've been infused with ShantiMari to create such an effect. That was the only thing Rhoane could imagine because everyone knew mermaids were only myths. Like darathi eneari and the sea king, they didn't exist.

Faelara tapped his shoulder and he turned toward two massive doors as they swung inward to reveal a huge hall covered in the decorative tiles, from floor to walls to ceiling. Flowers, stars, the sea, forests, deserts—every aspect of Summerlands life was captured in the room. Across the great vaulted ceiling was a blanket of midnight, with the sun at one end and twin moons at the other. In the direct center was Dal Tara.

A thrill shot through him at the sight of his mother's resting place. Although it was only colored glass, the artist had infused the mosaic with a touch of ShantiMari, which gave the portrait ethereal appeal.

At the far end of the room, two chairs sat upon a dais, with the king and queen looking as though they'd stepped from the ceiling. Queen Prateeni wore an elaborate headdress made of gold and gems. Exquisite strands of pearls framed her face. When she inclined her head in greeting, the sound of bells filled the space. Despite the heat, a thick blanket covered her body—its white fur shimmered against the queen's burnished skin.

Beside her, the king wore a less ostentatious crown, although it was covered in pearls, diamonds, and rubies. His right hand rested over the queen's left, a simple gesture that piqued Rhoane's interest. Most nobility rarely showed public affection, his mother and father among them. To see the king gaze upon his queen with devotion in his deep-brown eyes charmed Rhoane.

Myrddin chatted amiably with the monarchs as Rhoane and Faelara stood silently behind him. By the casual language and length to which he spoke, it became obvious the mage was a frequent visitor to the palace. Again, Rhoane and Faelara shared a questioning glance. The queen tilted her head in their direction, as if reminding the mage there were others in the room. Myrddin finished his tale and hooked a thumb at them.

"As promised, I brought you the two most gifted healers in all the realms. They will see your child delivered without incident. The Summerlands will have an heir in short order."

Faelara's amber eyes flashed anger toward the mage, her lips thinned to a dangerous white line.

"You are both *genari?*" Queen Prateeni asked. Rhoane had never heard the expression, and with the queen's heavily accented Elennish, he wasn't even sure whether she'd asked or stated a fact.

"No, Your Majesty. I am Lady Faelara dal Arran. My father is High Priest of Talaith, and while I am skilled in healing, I am not *genari.* Neither is my friend." Faelara cast a scathing glance at Myrddin, who smiled with a little too much mischief lurking in his eyes and upon his lips. "May I present Prince Rhoane, First Son of the Eleri."

Rhoane bowed low to the monarchs, his hand over his heart. Whatever was happening in the throne room, he wanted answers as much as Faelara did, but he chose to remain silent until he had the situation sorted.

The queen clapped a hand over her mouth as an audible gasp escaped her lips. "An Eleri? Here?" She rose on unstable legs, and her husband immediately was at her side to help her down the few steps. Her belly, naked and swollen with her growing child, protruded above the waistband of her long skirt. A swirl of golden dots had been carefully painted onto her skin.

"Welcome, Prince Rhoane, Lady Faelara. I am Queen

Prateeni, and this is my husband, King Faisal. But I'm sure you already know this. By the looks on your faces, I am going to guess you didn't know you were coming here to assist in the birth of our son."

The king placed a protective hand over Prateeni's belly. "She waited for your arrival, but our son is impatient. We were beginning to worry you would not be in time." His dark eyes bore into Faelara's. "Your empress assured me you were skilled in childbirth. This has been a difficult pregnancy for my wife. We cannot lose another child."

"Another?" Faelara ventured. "How many have there been?"

"Two thus far. Both male and in my final months." Prateeni's skin turned a horrible shade of ash, and Faelara reached for the woman's temple.

"You are like ice. Help me get her to her rooms. Rhoane, come with me." Faelara spit out orders faster than a hemlox did vinegar seeds. The others in the room moved into action, heeding every command the petite woman made.

Myrddin caught Rhoane's elbow as he strode past. "Don't be angry with me, boy. I did what I had to do to get you here."

"Why the deception? You could have just asked us to attend her birth."

"And would you have come?"

Rhoane knew the truth without saying the words. He wouldn't have traveled across the sea to help the queen, but manipulating them, as Myrddin had, deserved his wrath. "I suppose we are not to search for the *Darennsai's* sire, nor are we going to the other kingdoms, then?"

"Only if you want to do some sightseeing." Myrddin clapped him on the back. A grin teased his lips. "I know you spent more than three seasons with the Ullans, healing their sick, attending the wounded. You can do this, Rhoane. If the queen can give birth to one healthy child, she will never have difficulties again. It's imperative to her House that she deliver this baby."

Rhoane suppressed his anger. Myrddin had manipulated them and although he in time might understand why, he couldn't let the queen suffer now. "I will do this, for the queen and not for you. But you must promise me, no more lies. If you need my assistance, you ask for it. If you use cunning in the form of lies again, I will not view you as a friend. Am I understood?"

Myrddin faced him, a sober expression on his face. "You are a man of honor, Prince Rhoane. I don't wish to be your enemy." He held out his arm for Rhoane to grip, and the two embraced with the pact. "Now, see to the queen, will you? I have an errand to run."

Rhoane debated for a split second whether he should follow the mage, but Prateeni's screams pulled his attention to the royal bedchamber.

The scene he walked into was one of horror. A pool of blood ran slick across the floor, with footprints smeared from one end to the other. The queen thrashed atop the covers, mumbling incoherently. Faelara sat by her side, speaking in soothing tones. The king paced the room, his face a thunderstorm of emotions. When he saw Rhoane, he approached, lashing out as he did.

"You! You brought this on. What sort of charlatan are you? An Eleri prince? Ha! And where is Myrddin? He promised to be here for the birth. Why has he deserted my queen when he promised to help?"

Startled and confused by the tirade, Rhoane refused to shrink from the man. "I am not now, nor will I ever be, a charlatan. I have skill in healing, but if you would prefer I let your wife die, I will leave this room and never return. Her death will be on your conscience, Your Majesty, not mine."

The king fumed anew. Words spoken in his native tongue sputtered from his lips. Curses, most likely. Rhoane waited out the tantrum. His thoughts spun. What in Ohlin's name did Myrddin get them into? Thrusting them into an impossible situation with the queen. Declaring Rhoane and Faelara wouldn't be searching the other kingdoms, then who would? Myrddin? Whatever game the empress was playing, Rhoane wanted no part, but just as he had to endure Amdi's arena, he suspected he'd have to endure Lliandra's folly.

"Your Highness, please. Rhoane and I can deliver this child, but you must contain your worry. Yelling at the Eleri prince will not help your wife." Faelara's sharp tone silenced the king.

With a deep scowl and quick nod to the bed, Faisal pleaded, "If you can help her, I would be grateful." He grabbed Rhoane's sleeve as he passed. "But speak to me like that again, and I will not be as generous." Whether he meant Rhoane or Faelara was not immediately clear. Rhoane suspected both.

He met the man's even stare. "You cannot force respect, sire. It must be earned. I will forgive your outburst this time and look forward to your future generosity." He hadn't spent all his time with the Ullans without learning how to stare down an enemy. Except Rhoane didn't think Faisal was his adversary. He hoped the king felt the same. They needed to be allies, the Summerlands king and the Eleri.

Faisal glared at him, his lips moving in silent rebuke. Rhoane brushed past to the queen's bed. Sweat soaked the pillowcase beneath Prateeni's head, and her garments were stained with blood. Her distended belly protruded at grotesque angles where the baby fought against his mother's movements.

Without speaking, Rhoane channeled his ShantiMari and focused on the ancient practices of calm he'd learned as a young man. He spread his hands wide over the woman's body and gently let his power embrace her. She paused in her thrashing, and Rhoane cooed reminders to relax, to think of the baby. He sent subtle suggestions of sleep to both her and the child. Only when her body relaxed into the thick blankets did Rhoane place his palms upon her belly. Eyes closed, he probed her womb to look for signs of distress. The baby's heartbeat entwined with his power, faint but steady. If they didn't bring the child forth within the next bell, both mother and son would die.

"Faelara, reach inside and tell me what you feel," Rhoane whispered.

"Are you mad? The king will behead us both for impropriety."

He'd known Faelara less than two moonturns, not long enough to be sure he could trust her, but the situation didn't allow for caution. He lifted his hands from the queen's inert body and brought them together at his chest. Kaleigh's image formed in his mind, and he recited the words she'd spoken to him hundreds of times. The cadence had to be perfect. The words spoken in the right order. There could be no hesitation.

The others in the room slowed to an unrecognizable pace. Faelara looked up at him with wonder in her eyes. "Are you doing this?"

"Please, do not ever tell anyone what you witness here today."

"You have my word." She touched a sunbeam that traveled from the window, her look one of pure awe. With a flick of her finger, she sent the ray spiraling in the opposite direction. "How is this possible?"

"An Eleri gift few are granted." He indicated the woman on the bed, "We must focus our powers and save two lives. The queen is fading as well as her babe." A glint of indecision crossed her eyes. "What is it, Faelara?"

"Can they hear us?"

He shook his head. "We are nothing but an irritating buzz. If there is something I should know, you must tell me."

"It's just…doesn't it seem strange the queen went into labor not more than a few minutes after we arrived? By the looks of her, she isn't due for a few weeks, possibly a moonturn."

"Do you think Myrddin had anything to do with it?" The man was a mystery to Rhoane, a fact he was determined to change.

"Only if it served his purpose. He's a scoundrel to be sure, but utterly devoted to Lliandra. I suppose now he'll want me to stay here and care for the queen." She cocked her head to the side. A silly grin tilted her lips. "That sly fox. He managed to get me away from Talaith *and* removed me from the distasteful business of finding Lliandra's lover. I owe him a debt of thanks."

Whereas Rhoane had lashed out at the man, Faelara gave him gratitude. Once more, he was humbled by her kindness. It also softened his feelings for the mage. Perhaps his manipulations did serve a purpose. Still, he didn't like being deceived.

"Now, to deliver this child." Faelara snapped her fingers, and a bowl of steaming water appeared. She scrubbed her hands and forearms before drying them on a towel. When she'd finished, she waved the basin away and settled herself between the queen's legs.

"Perhaps I am not the only one with secrets," Rhoane said, impressed with her ease in wielding ShantiMari.

Faelara's grin turned to determination as she maneuvered her hand into the birthing canal. Rhoane kept his eyes diverted to protect the queen's modesty, focusing instead on the protruding belly. His power swirled within the womb, healing what he sensed had been harmed with the queen's fit. The baby's heartbeat faltered for a moment, and Rhoane urged Faelara to hurry.

The queen groaned, and the sound echoed off his folding of time.

"I can feel the baby's head," Faelara said. "He's turned, which is very good for us. Can you get him to drop down?"

Rhoane shifted his power to both the baby and Prateeni. "I need you to push, Your Majesty." He wasn't at all sure she could hear him, but when he felt her contract and push against his power, relief crashed over him. They had a chance of delivering not just the baby from danger, but the mother as well.

"That's good, Rhoane. Have her push again, but not yet. I need to shift his shoulders. He's too broad for her." Faelara jerked and shoved against the queen, grunting her dissatisfaction with each thrust. "Push. Now."

Rhoane repeated his request, and Prateeni responded. From the corner of his eye, Rhoane saw the faintest shadow approaching. He turned toward it, but sunlight poured through the window and blotted out the stain.

"He's almost through, Rhoane. Undo whatever it was you did. We can't deliver the child without them seeing us."

Rhoane released his hold over time and swayed with the rush of power sucked from him. The king stood beside him, holding Prateeni's hand and begging her to fight. At the sight of Faelara and the baby's head, tears glistened in his eyes.

"One more push, Queen Prateeni. You can do it," Faelara urged, as if she'd been asking the queen to assist with the birth the whole time.

With a deafening cry, the queen bore down. A moment later, her son slipped onto the bed. Rhoane's ShantiMari engulfed the lad, sustaining his weakened heart, forcing air into his lungs. He gave a lusty wail, and the room breathed as if for the first time all day. Happy sobs filled the air with bells peeling from the palace to the harbor. Between hiccup-laced cries of joy and intermittent winces of pain, the queen thanked Faelara and Rhoane for their assistance. Even the king sobbed his gratitude when he saw his son. The fierce ruler became a doting father in the space of a breath.

Faelara covered the queen and worked her healing while Rhoane stood back, splitting his ShantiMari between the queen and the baby. He'd witnessed births before, but never this intimately. Something inside him shifted. A curious little tilt to his heart that he couldn't explain. After so much death in Amdi's arena, he'd worked to bring life into the world.

Once the child had been cleaned and swaddled, mother and son were moved to another room until her bedchamber could be cleaned. Rhoane, Faelara, and the king stayed with them well into the night, each curled in an overstuffed chair trying to stay vigilant. Eventually their eyelids drooped and sleep won out.

Just before he drifted off, Rhoane cast his power over the bed chamber to add one final ward against the blackness he sensed at the edge of his consciousness. His ShantiMari blanketed them, and he snuggled beneath it in the knowledge they would be safe. A shock of white filled his vision for a moment, then disappeared.

A woman's voice lingered in his dreams. *Be gone, demon.*

CHAPTER TEN

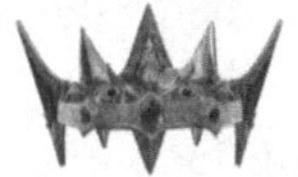

Sunlight warmed his skin, and Rhoane awoke on the sofa feeling as though he'd been trampled by a vorlock. He cricked his neck from one side to the other and stretched his back at the same time. The room was empty except for the queen, who rested atop the massive bed. The newborn prince suckled at her breast. Prateeni watched him with the steady patience of a levon tracking its prey.

Rhoane glanced away, embarrassed.

"Come here, Prince Rhoane," the queen's hoarse whisper commanded.

He did as told, still trying to avert his eyes from the intimacy of her child's feeding.

"Does this make you uncomfortable? A mother giving nourishment to her young?"

"It is not proper for me to see you in a state of undress, Your Majesty."

"Are all Eleri as uptight as you?"

Rhoane flashed her a warning look.

"Ah. They are. I apologize. Here, I am covered now. Your

delicate Eleri senses will not be offended." She draped a gauzy cloth over herself and the baby's head.

"I meant no offense. I merely thought you would like some privacy."

"I know what you thought. Sit. I want to discuss something with you."

Rhoane looked for a seat, finding none other than the pair they'd slept in, and sat where she indicated upon the bed, although at a discreet enough distance should anyone enter they would not think him being inappropriate, yet close enough the queen would not reprimand him.

"I want to thank you for saving our lives last night." She placed a hand over her abdomen. "I can feel you, in here." At Rhoane's widened eyes, she explained. "Your ShantiMari—it is powerful in healing. I heard you and your lady. Begging me to remain calm, telling me when to breathe, when to push."

"Faelara and I were worried about you."

"Not Lady Faelara. The other one. A woman of immeasurable beauty with raven locks that swept past her arse. She looks like you, even."

Rhoane's heart sputtered in this throat, choking off air.

"Did I say something to upset you? Why are you looking at me as if I were a shadow walker?"

"Did this woman have a name?"

"None that she shared with me. Why? Who is she?"

Rhoane took a long breath and glanced to the ceiling, willing his eyes to dry. "I believe the woman you saw was my mother, Aislinn. She moved beyond the veils the day I left the Narthvier." He returned his gaze to the queen.

Prateeni leaned against the headboard, her face a placard of emotions. "I am truly sorry for your loss, Your Highness."

The prince's little hands clutched at air while he nursed. He made happy little mewing sounds much like a kitten's. The scarf slipped from the queen and Rhoane smoothed the baby's full head of curls, shocked at how soft he was. Rhoane had assisted in several births but had never held a child in his arms. Not even his younger siblings. They were always given to nursemaids after birth. He fought a strong compulsion to take the child from his mother and cradle him close. To protect him.

His eyes met Prateeni's. "You feed your own child. Do you not have a wet nurse?"

"I nearly died bringing him into this world. Do you think I'm going to let someone else raise him? He is my son, and I shall be a part of every accomplishment and trial he has until he's old enough to reign on his own." A blush of pride swept over her cheeks. "My mother did the same for me. It's only right I am there for my children."

"Is it tradition for Summerlands women to be this involved?"

"I don't know about tradition, but it's what makes sense. Wouldn't you agree? Why go through the trouble to have them if you aren't going to raise them?" She shifted her position, and the baby let out a cry of displeasure. "Shh, little one. There is more." She settled him against her other breast and smiled when he curled his tiny fingers over her own. "I should like to walk in the garden when he is fed. The sun always lifts my spirits."

"You need to rest. Your body suffered great shock and injury last night. It will do no one good for you to collapse from exhaustion."

"You healed me, remember?"

"I healed your womb. Even that needs time to recover."

"I am healthy. Check for yourself if you don't believe me." She took his hand as if to place it over her heart. Rhoane pulled away, but she chided, "It's only a breast, Rhoane. It won't bite. Now don't be ridiculous, feel my pulse. Tell me I'm not strong enough."

She placed his hand firmly on her chest. He was certain the pounding he felt was his own heartbeat and not hers. Even with the women Amdi had thrown his way, Rhoane had never touched them. His healing was always done at a distance, nothing upon the body proper.

"My dear prince, are you going to declare me fit, or are you not?"

Rhoane kept his hand steady and focused on the queen's heart. It fluttered with a consistency he admired. Strong, healthy, powerful. She was indeed fit. He shifted his attention to the rest of her body, examining the bones and muscles. "May I?" He placed his hands upon her shoulders.

"Look at you. One touch of my breast, and you can't resist."

Rhoane immediately snatched his hands away.

"Oh, for the love of gods, touch me. I get no more thrill from this than you." She closed her eyes, a saucy smile on her lips. Rhoane hesitated, unsure whether she jested or not. The desire to clinically observe her recovery was too great. He pressed his fingertips to her forehead and sent a thread of his power through her mind, avoiding her thoughts. His hands continued down her cheeks to her throat, where he paused while she swallowed. Satisfied, he slid past her clavicle to her shoulders and over her arms. Touch greatly magnified his ability to sense abnormalities within the body. Her blood pumped steadily through her veins, making a tiny rushing sound in his mind.

When he came to her midsection, he hesitated once more, but she clucked her tongue, and he resumed his examination. Her womb suffered still, but his ShantiMari continued to knit together where trauma had occurred. She would fully recover in time, but needed to be careful.

"You are gentle, like your mother," Prateeni murmured. "I can sense her in your power."

Rhoane glanced at the queen, who watched him with steady interest.

"She gave you a wonderful gift, Prince Rhoane. Strength and kindness, yes, but she gave something of much greater value. Her death gave you freedom."

"How do you figure?"

"I know of the oracles and prophecies surrounding the Eirielle. The one your own Verdaine calls *Darennsai*. You are destined for her, but you are not tied to those prophecies in the way you believe. You still have power over your own future." She leaned forward and touched his shoulder. A shock of her Mari sliced through him, startling him in its intensity. "You wear your anger like a badge, daring anyone to get too close. There is no reason for this rage."

He started to argue, but she was right. He'd been nursing his ire since he was a lad. Believing he'd been forced into the oath and the loss of choice. He'd welcomed the battles in Ulla. They were his punishment. His eternal suffering for what he'd done to his mother.

A door opened, and the king's voice bellowed into the room, "What in Julieta's name is going on in here?"

Rhoane stared, dumbstruck, at the monarch. He'd forgotten his hands were still on the queen's calves. Myrddin followed close behind, that damned mischievousness dancing in his eyes.

"The prince was having his way with me," Prateeni said matter-of-factly. The king fumed, his face turning eight shades of red in the space of a heartbeat. "Darling, please. Rhoane was making sure I'm fit to leave this bed, nothing more."

Rhoane removed his hands from the queen. "You may walk in the garden, but not for long. You are still healing."

Myrddin approached the bed and reached for the little prince. "May I?" He cuddled the boy against his bearded chin, cooing like an over-proud grandfather. "He is strong as can be. You did a fine job, Your Majesty."

Faelara joined them and waited patiently for her turn to hold the baby. After everyone finished with their kisses and cuddles, the queen retired to her dressing room to change before her stroll in the garden. Faelara led Rhoane to his suite of rooms, where a lavish meal had been laid out for him. He grazed on the delicious food, musing on what the queen had said to him.

His mother's death had freed him.

From what? The constraints of Eleri life? Certainly not his obligation to his goddess. He shredded a piece of bread without thought. Prateeni had said she'd read oracles and prophecies about the Eirielle, and the empress had mentioned her as well. He needed to know everything they did about the girl. If he was to be bound to her, he would be well served to know what Aelinae expected of his Darennsai.

A cluster of young women, all dressed in the skimpy skirts and tops of the Summerlands, giggled as they passed his doors that led to the inner courtyard of the palace. Someone had left the double glass doors open, which gave the women a glimpse into Rhoane's rooms. It was possible his Darennsai might someday come from the very child he had helped bring into the world. Although something told him she would not.

"Is your meal that bad?"

Rhoane jerked his attention away from the window and his musings. "I did not hear you knock."

"I imagine you didn't. May I join you?" Myrddin took a seat opposite Rhoane before he'd consented. "I'm sorry I wasn't here last night to assist with the birth. I thought we had more time. Time is a funny thing, is it not? You always think you have more than you really do. Except for when forced to wait—then there is too much time." He pushed his palms against his forehead. "If you really want to know, I visited a spice merchant in the city and had him make up two potions. One for healing the queen, the other for easing her passing."

"You were unsure she would survive the ordeal. But you told me this child must live. The future of her House depended on it. I assumed it had something to do with the *Darennsai.*"

"I wish I knew the future, Rhoane. I've found it useful to prepare for every situation. When you've lived as long as I have, you learn not to get too attached. The king and queen, they're good people. Loving, kind, decent rulers who want the best for their subjects. I sometimes wish Lliandra could be more like them, but she is who she is. She was shaped by a tradition dating back to the beginning of Aelinae. As were Faisal and Prateeni, and every other ruler. Each taking a different path to what essentially becomes the same end point."

His gaze traveled to the now empty courtyard. A throaty resonance entered his tone. "It's time those traditions were remade. That's why I think Aelinae needs the Eirielle. Some say she will destroy Aelinae; others say she's the savior. In the end, it will come down to her."

"You think I will have something to do with her decision."

"You will have everything to do with it." Myrddin bit into a piece of fruit, ignoring the juices that ran down his chin and through his beard. Three more bites were consumed before he wiped his face with his sleeve. "The king wants to go riding with you this afternoon."

Rhoane hedged. The abrupt change of topic clouded his thinking. "Will you join us?" The idea of spending the day with Faisal didn't bring joy to his heart.

"I'm afraid not. I have business in the city and preparations for my departure."

"We are leaving? So soon after the birth of the prince?"

"I'm leaving. You and Faelara are staying until you feel the queen's health is not at risk."

Rhoane didn't tell him the queen was fit. He debated asking whether there was another reason they were being left behind, but held back. Whatever reasons the empress had for sending Myrddin alone were hers. Truth be told, he didn't relish the thought of continuing their search for his betrothed's father. He would much rather stay and get to know the Summerlands queen. She'd intrigued him with her words and he desperately wanted to understand what she'd meant.

"Lliandra wants me to ride west to Danuri, and then Caer Idris." Myrddin broke into his thoughts. "Now that you have left the vier, events will happen quickly. The Eirielle's father must be a perfect match for Lliandra, which means highborn with strength in ShantiMari. The Lord of the Dark is blissfully wed with an heir of eight seasons but Lliandra's heard he has a cousin who might be a proper match for her. I've been instructed to deliver him to Talaith."

"I do not envy you this journey, but appreciate you allowing Lady Faelara and myself to care for the queen and her child."

"Ride with Faisal. Get to know him as a king, a father, and a man. I think you will be surprised by what you discover."

Myrddin's cryptic words piqued his interest. "I promise you, I shall." Perhaps Faisal was not the bellowing tyrant Rhoane thought him to be.

As it turned out, away from the palace, Faisal was relaxed and genial, although Rhoane could see the strain that worry placed upon him. The king fretted over his wife and child, but Rhoane assured him they were healthy.

They rode to the edge of a massive forest and instead of being homesick, Rhoane felt conflicted at the sight of lush flowers and flowing vines.

"What do you make of our Hben Firn?" Faisal said with a wide smile. "Not as expansive as your Narthvier, but just as lovely, no?"

"It is much different from where I was raised." Thick air heavy with moisture surrounded them, and Rhoane was tempted to remove his tunic.

"The firn sustains us by providing medicinal plants and food, as well as giving protection against flood, erosion, and drought. We owe our lives to the firn." Faisal tipped his fingers to his forehead and circled them downward with a flourish. *"Archainea edahmi etoru."*

Vines from the nearest tree reached toward the king and caressed his cheek.

Rhoane stared in amazement at the interaction. He'd been raised to believe only the Eleri interacted with nature.

"You are surprised, no?" The king bellowed a laugh and patted Rhoane on the back. "Let's see what else makes your eyes widen." He rode off, his laughter floating on the air.

The choice of Faisal's wording wasn't lost on Rhoane. Yes, he'd been surprised, just as Myrddin had predicted. As he urged Lucitan to catch up to the king, he wondered what else the Summerlands ruler could show him and found himself unexpectedly anxious to find out.

A few days later, Rhoane and Faelara said their farewells to Myrddin and he unobtrusively left the palace. As Rhoane watched the mage amble down the cobbled road toward the harbor, he wished him well on his hunt. For that's what it truly was—a hunt for the perfect specimen. It mattered not if Lliandra loved her mate, as long as he could produce a worthy heir. Rhoane shook his head. Pity lodged in his throat. He hoped when the Darennsai learned of their pairing, she would view him as more than an obligation.

Faisal beckoned Rhoane to join him, and for a moment, Rhoane envied the king. In one arm he held his tiny son, while the other draped casually over the shoulders of his wife. Their expressions were twin beacons of love. The rage in Rhoane's throat gagged him. It was no longer for the empress, but for his unsuspecting future mate. She, like him, never had a choice.

The king and queen cooed over their child, adoration flowing from their words. Rhoane swallowed hard, but couldn't dissolve his anger. The queen was wrong—he would never be free. He was in bondage to his goddess. He would never know love like the king and queen shared. He stormed past the monarchs, ignoring their surprised gasps.

Somehow, he'd convinced himself the image of the silver-haired vixen was real and that she would one day love him. At that moment, with Myrddin abandoning him in a strange land, and his path uncertain, he needed something to distract him. If the mage was right, it would be a long time before the Darennsai was even born, longer still until she came of age. Rhoane had to find something to fill his days while he waited. He couldn't waste time pining for a love of his own. At the very least, he needed to be useful, to fill his days with work that eliminated any opportunities for worrying over what couldn't be.

Love was for people like Faisal and Prateeni. Rhoane needed none of it. What he required—no, what Aelinae required—was for him to be the Darennsai's equal. But how? How was he expected to be the protector and guardian of a goddess?

He glanced at the colorful murals in the palace's corridors and had an overwhelming sense of being trapped. He needed to think. To breathe. To be free, if only for one day.

Lucitan galloped along the southeastern shores of the Summerlands, having left Menurra far behind. Rhoane had ridden through orchards and vineyards, past fields where workers toiled in the midday heat, but here on the beach, there wasn't another soul to be found. For one wild moment, Rhoane dreamt of living out the rest of his days hidden away from the rest of the world.

The coastline had many caves, certainly one was habitable. Except Rhoane hated water. He would never survive so near the sea. A cave in the mountains or near the Narthvier would be ideal.

Rhoane wore an impish grin as he dismounted and unfastened Luc's girth. What an idea. He, First Son of the Eleri, a hermit. Penniless, living truly exiled, away from everyone. He tilted his face to the sun, drawing its warmth to his core. Could he? Dare he even think it? He placed the saddle and bridle on a patch of hard sand far from the surf and patted Luc's flank. "Go on, boy. Graze on the tall grasses, but don't drink the water." Luc snorted and trotted off, shaking his head and bucking his back legs.

Rhoane removed his boots and rolled his linen breeches up to his knees before settling onto the sand. His thoughts crashed in time to the waves. *Isolation. Obligation. Prophecy. Duty. Honor.* He shut off his mind and focused on his surroundings. The repetitiveness of the waves was like a lullaby to his stretched nerves. He lay back, propped on his elbows, and stared at the sea. There was symmetry to the water's movements, and he wondered what made some water roil, like the surf of the sea, and some water placid, like lakes.

His spontaneous laughter frightened nearby birds that scavenged the shoreline. Those thoughts were better left for men like Brandt. Men who studied the stars. Not an Eleri who, until recently, had never seen moving water larger than a river. To think, four seasons earlier he had no desire to understand the world beyond the Narthvier, and here he was, contemplating the ways of the terrarae and skies. Despite his belief that men like Brandt were far better equipped to answer his musings, the need to know more drilled into his psyche. The lad who had left the vier remained within him, but he'd grown beyond that boy's existence and sought to discover more about Aelinae, what lay beyond the stars, and what he himself was capable of. He was more than Amdi's fighter. More than Prateeni's *genari.* More even, than simply the fated one of the Darennsai. But what, exactly, was he?

The sun warmed him into a tranquil state. He was tired of being angry, of questioning what was right, and he was more than tired of having the same debate over and over again within his mind. No matter how he approached the argument, he came no closer to finding a solution to his situation. Was he being too impatient, not allowing the future to unfold as he'd been told, but trying to force his desires on destiny?

He touched the hilt of his sword. Verdaine had told him he'd know the Darennsai by her own sword. But where was it? And where was she? If Lliandra was to be her mother, who then, the father? How long must he wait for her? Eleri lived hundreds of seasons; perhaps he should find a cave and wait until destiny caught up to him.

The idea was amusing, but impractical. Even so, he couldn't shake the feeling more was expected of him. Surely he wasn't to sit around and do nothing while waiting. A shadow fell over him and he squinted in the bright sunlight. The woman with eyes as blue as the deepest sea appeared before him. Her long, silvery hair floated on the breeze. She wore no clothing but was covered in stars, as if beneath her skin the very sky existed. She laughed, and it was the sweetest sound he'd ever heard. Full of hope and promises.

"Always be curious," she teased. "Never accept that what you see is all there is." Her accented voice touched his heart and embedded itself into his very marrow. "Take risks, make mistakes, and get messy. Be brave, and do what frightens you most, but always, always have hope, my beloved." She bent as if to caress his cheek, and a warm breeze swept over his skin. Her lips pressed to his with surprising solidness.

All too soon, their lips parted.

"Who are you?" He breathed the words, afraid any sound might frighten her away.

She laughed once more and stepped back. "I am yours, mi carae. Forever."

Before he could ask her where he would find her, Lucitan galloped up the shore, spraying water with each pound of his hooves. In an instant, he tore through the image, and Rhoane screamed at him to stop, but the woman was gone. Only the scent of jasmine and sea air remained.

He sat upright and glared at his horse. Luc gazed back with indifference, then turned suddenly and trotted into the surf.

"You stupid beast, come here at once." Luc's coat dripped

from his shenanigans, and Rhoane cursed him under his breath. "We have no time for these games. Come. Here."

Luc lowered his head to the surf, gathering water in his lips and showering Rhoane with it. If he didn't know better, he'd think the stallion was challenging him. He paced the shore for a quarter bell, trying everything to coax his horse out of the water. Luc would prance and trot in circles, flip his mane and tail, spray water, or paw at the surf, but he never came a pace closer to the shore.

Irritated at the beast, but more so at the ridiculousness of his fear of water, Rhoane finally stripped off his breeches and shirt, cursing the entire time. As he stood on the shore in nothing but his smallclothes, he glared at Lucitan. "See what you have done? You are forcing me into the water. Are you happy now?"

Luc whinnied and tossed his head.

"This is ludicrous. I should sell you to the Artagh. They will make a nice meal of you, no doubt." He plunged into the surf and fought the panic that swept up his spine. When the waves crashed around his knees, he paused long enough to battle a wave of nausea. Luc eyed him warily, but did not back away.

Six more steps, and Rhoane was beside his horse, gasping. The turquoise water lapping at his legs was warm, not at all menacing. He rested his head against the stallion's neck and let his heart rate return to normal. The longer he stood there, the more comfortable he became. *Take risks. Make mistakes.* That's what the vision had told him.

She'd also again called him her beloved.

Luc nudged him, and Rhoane's laughter bubbled up from deep inside. How asinine he must look standing thigh-deep in the surf, almost naked, and leaning against his horse for support. He pulled himself atop Luc's back and tilted his face to the sky. *Be brave, and do what frightens you most, but always, always have hope.*

Rhoane nudged Luc into a trot, and together they raced

along the shore until they were soaked. With each thunderous crash of Luc's hooves, Rhoane released his fear, his anger, his well-honed rage. Twice the beauty had shown herself to him when he needed her most. Like faerie drossfire during the darkest days of Wintertide, she staved off the blackness that threatened his sanity. Both times there was gaiety in her eyes and laughter upon her lips. If she were his Darennsai, she didn't appear to resent the obligation.

And if she wasn't his Darennsai? What if she was a vision meant to lure him astray?

He stopped the thoughts that nudged at his tentative calm. Whoever she was, and come what may, he welcomed her company. An idea, impossible as it seemed, seeded itself into his mind. He always had a choice. As a young lad, he could've declined his goddess's request. At the edge of the Narthvier, he chose to ride east, to Ulla. And now, he could choose to love the Darennsai or simply be her protector.

Rhoane knew it was far too late for that. He was indelibly in love with her already. Real or imagined, she was his lady and would be until he took his dying breath. He recalled the vows he'd given Verdaine all those seasons ago when he was just a lad, adding to the oath.

"I, Rhoane, will never know another but the Darennsai, should she wish it. If she does not, I will remain untouched, refusing to share my body with another. My sword, my life, my love will forever be hers." A flash of white crested the horizon and Rhoane squinted to better see from whence it came. Another flash rose high into the air, disappearing behind the blazing sun. "If she sees fit to love me in return," he said to the waves, "I will do all in my power to keep her safe and never cause her harm. This I swear."

To make an oath such as this felt like he should be kneeling or touching his sword or *something*, but there was only him and Luc. And the vast ocean. They were his witnesses. Rhoane cocked his head and grinned. The sun and moon and stars bore witness to his oath as well. "This I swear!" His voice bellowed over the water and with it, the last dredges of his rage spiraled away from his heart. At last, he was ready to accept what was to come. Not just accept it—challenge it, embrace it, and shape it. His path was his to forge. No one else's.

He and Lucitan chased waves and galloped along the shore until the sun hovered over the cliffs to the east. Luc brought them back to where they'd left their belongings and trotted to a stop, his chest heaving with the exciting ride. Rhoane's heart pounded against his ribs. There he was, an Eleri riding an Ullan stallion on a deserted Summerlands beach. How vain he'd been. How positively self-righteous. He'd been raised to believe the Eleri were above all Fadair, but what if no one culture was above another? Only the gods were exalted above all. And someday the Darennsai would reside in Dal Tara with his goddess, Verdaine. With a start, he realized all along he'd had it wrong—she didn't have to be good enough for him—he must be good enough for her.

He slid from the stallion, sore from the ride, hungry, and sunburned, but he didn't care. His mood was lighter than it had been in far too long. The setting sun cast long shadows over the beach, and he shivered against the encroaching chill. That morning when he left the palace, he'd ridden in a daze. Now he was unsure of the path he'd taken to the beach. Trying to find his way back to Menurra at night would be suicide. There was nothing for it but to don his clothing and search for driftwood.

Once he had a fire made, he stretched out on the hard sand and fell into a deep sleep. He dreamt not of the platinum-haired woman, but of myths—of the merfolk and their king. They swam with him beneath the sea to a palace made of coral with alabaster columns and spirals of whalebone. The king welcomed him, calling him by name.

"Come," the sea king said, "I will tell you a tale."

Rhoane swam with the king to a vast room where other merfolk waited. He was not afraid in his dream, but excited. Anxious to hear the tale, Rhoane rested with the king's daughters on soft plants that tickled his skin.

"Long ago," the king's voice was low, but reached clear to the back of the enclosure, "before the merfolk and even the Eleri existed, there was only terrarae and sky. In the heavens, lived the Darennsai. She was beautiful beyond compare, with moonstone and stardust making up her form. To gaze at her was to see the entire vastness of this world and those beyond."

Rhoane twitched in his sleep, remembering the silver-haired vision had appeared to have all the stars of the sky beneath her skin.

"Upon the terrarae, there lived a young sapling, the Surtentse. He dwelled alone, nurturing his plants and tending his gardens. Each day and night they would gaze at each other, never touching or speaking, but knowing in their hearts they were destined to be as one."

"I love this story." One of the younger mermaid princesses sighed. Her vibrant blue hair floated around her impish face and he thought he saw the faintest touch of Glamour beneath her skin.

"One day," the sea king continued, "unable to bear the separation any longer, the Darennsai plummeted to the terrarae and her certain death. The sapling did what anyone in love would do —he sprouted wings. He stretched his branches and leaves until he flew to meet her and captured the Darennsai just in time. They tumbled together into the sea, where something extraordinary happened. They grew arms and legs, torsos and faces. They became man and woman."

A collective sigh went up from the merfolk, making bubbles rise above their heads. It didn't occur to Rhoane that he shouldn't be able to breathe underwater because he knew it was only a dream and in dreams anything was possible.

King Baldev paused before finishing the story. A sad little smile tugged at his lips. Bittersweet in its simplicity. "There, in the warm waters of the Summerlands sea, they swam together and consummated their love. But when the Surtentse stepped out of the water, he became a sapling once more. Shocked and frightened, he returned to the safety of the water where he once more was a man. Night came and there was no moon; no stars lit the dark sky, and they quaked with fright, knowing if the Darennsai was not returned to the sky, life on Aelinae would cease to exist."

"What did she do?" the young blue-haired princess asked.

The sea king smiled at his daughter, who very likely knew the end of the tale. "She did what was right for Aelinae and returned to her heavenly home, and the Surtentse returned to the terrarae, where once more he became a sapling."

Rhoane woke with a start. For one mad moment he thought he saw tiny branches stretched from his skin, each with a single leaf. Embers from the fire glowed softly in the pre-dawn light. He sat up and shook his head to clear his thoughts. The dream lingered still, vivid in his mind, yet details slipped away. There was much more to the dream, to the story, but each time he reached for more, he remembered less.

A nagging disquiet lingered. Something the darathi eneari had told him, he was certain and yet it, too, escaped him.

His stomach gave a vicious tug, and he stumbled from his makeshift bed to the edge of the shoreline. He scooped a handful of water into his hands and brought it to his face. *Darathi eneari.* Again and again he splashed water over his face in an attempt to refresh his thinking. In his dream, there was a darathi eneari—a water dragon. He was certain of it. But they didn't exist. They were legends, nothing more.

For Ages, his people had been the Caretakers of the darathi vorsi and always there had been stories, folklore passed down about the water dragons, yet no one had seen them since before his people could remember. Since they shared a collective memory of past events, it was widely believed if the darathi eneari ever existed, it was too long ago to be of any concern.

Luc trotted to his side, and Rhoane gazed out over the horizon where the sun rose in the west. To some, the Darennsai was nothing but a legend, yet he believed she was real. If she could exist, then certainly so could merfolk and darathi eneari.

He saddled Luc and climbed atop his horse, his mind settled somewhere beneath the waves. The ride to Menurra was once clouded with possibilities. He returned to the palace before breakfast, but the place was already a hive of activity. Several clusters of men on horseback waited in the courtyard. Faelara marched toward a white mare, her face set into a hard line. When she glanced up and saw him, palpable relief swept over her features.

"Thank the gods! We thought you were kidnapped by pirates." She hurried to him, concern replacing her relief. "Rykoto's balls, Rhoane, what happened to you?"

A pinch of guilt twisted in his gut. She was worried about him. He surveyed the soldiers. Faisal was sending out a full regiment to search for him. How selfish he'd been to stay on the beach without letting the others know he was well. How idiotic to think no one would care.

"I am sorry, Faelara. I lost my way, and it became too dark to travel safely."

"You're sunburned. Come, let's get you fed and salved."

Faisal rushed from the palace with Prateeni not far behind, the prince held close to her breast. "Your Highness! Thank Julieta you are well." He indicated the mounted men. "I was ready to search the entire island for you."

Rhoane slid from Lucitan's back and bowed low to the king. "I hope you will accept my sincerest apologies. I did not mean to cause you alarm." He hadn't expected this much concern from the king, and it unbalanced him, to say the least. "I was able to see some of your beautiful kingdom on my spontaneous journey, and I hope you will allow me to stay for a while more. I feel there is much I can learn from you, great king."

Faisal looked taken aback by his statement, but then a shrewd smile lit up his face. "I would be most interested in hearing of your intrepid adventure. Come. As Lady Faelara said, you could use a hot meal and a bath. Afterwards, we will meet and have tea."

Queen Prateeni placed a hand on Rhoane's forearm and stood on tiptoe to kiss his cheek. "You frightened us, Prince Rhoane. Pirates ravage our coastline and would love to have a prince as their captive. You would raise a handsome ransom, I wager." Her lips lingered on his cheek, and he smelled her scent of honeysuckle mixed with the milky sweetness of the prince. His curls tickled Rhoane's chin.

"Again, I am sorry I caused you alarm. I promise, in the future I will take an escort when I wish to tour your kingdom."

A look of relief crossed her face, but there was something hidden in her eyes that put Rhoane on edge.

"What is it, Your Majesty?" he whispered. "Something unsettles you, and I do not think it was my absence."

"I am not unsettled," she admitted, speaking low enough only he could hear. She clutched her baby tighter and wound her free arm through Rhoane's. "I sense in you peace. Something happened to you last night that helped ease your troubled mind, and for that I am grateful. But there is more…elusive, yet there all the same."

Her ability to read him was uncanny. The disquiet he'd felt upon waking was what she sensed beneath his calm. On the ride back to Menurra, he'd remembered everything the darathi eneari had told him and immediately wished he hadn't.

In his dream, the king had called him Surtentse, beloved of the Darennsai. After the king's tale, the water dragon had told him the Darennsai was not yet born. His intended would be a child made of stars turned flesh. Her mother would be the Lady of Light and her father, the Lord of the Dark. Moonstone and stardust would color her hair and she would wield a sword of two dragons. She would love him with every breath, every touch, every thought. He would become her world, her reason for existing, and he would betray her. Not once, but twice.

Then he would kill her.

CHAPTER TWELVE

King Faisal paced the tile floor of his office, and Rhoane studied the man's movements. They'd dined on fresh seafood, drank several cups of tea, rehashed Rhoane's journey of the previous day until there was nothing left to dissect from his tale, and still the king was agitated.

Plans were being made for the naming day of the little prince, and Rhoane thought perhaps this worried the king, but Faisal waved off his suggestion to help with the preparations. The queen and child were in good health. Faelara had taken excellent care of the pair while Rhoane was gone, showing her skills at healing were equal to, if not greater than, his own. She'd mentioned in passing again that she might enjoy a trip to Ulla to study with their healers, but Rhoane had given a noncommittal reply. He wasn't certain she could handle the brutality of Amdi's kingdom.

"I have a proposition for you." Faisal pulled Rhoane from his thoughts. "Lady Faelara has requested an extended stay to care for the queen and prince, as well as to learn our ways and customs. She feels it would be of service to her own empress if the kingdoms shared resources, and I must say, I agree with her."

Rhoane stifled his surprise. First she'd asked him to take her to Ulla, and then she'd requested to stay in the Summerlands. Either she was intent on not returning to Talaith anytime soon, or she had an insatiable curiosity. He suspected it was the former and there might be a gentleman involved in her reluctance.

"I think opening negotiations for trade would benefit everyone," Rhoane offered. "It certainly would hurt the pirates' business of stealing your goods to sell on the mainland."

"I'm glad you mentioned that, Prince Rhoane. I've been wondering what I could do with an errant prince in my kingdom, and I believe Lady Faelara has given me an idea. I could use a man of your skill and upbringing. You survived Ulla's arena, which means you can fight, but I can teach you—other things."

Rhoane dragged his fingertips along the edge of his chin. He had nowhere to be until the Darennsai was born. "Other things?"

"I'd like to propose, shall we say, a clandestine arrangement." The king gazed at Rhoane with narrowed eyes, his lips pursed beneath his thick beard.

"You want me to spy for you?"

"Spy is such an ugly word. You are *sheanna*, which means you are a man without a kingdom. You are beholden to no ruler. I don't ask you to spy for me, but I do ask that you become an agent for all of Aelinae. I have men who can teach you to blend into a crowd until you are as good as invisible. They will train you to fight with stealth, not for survival, but with grace. They will show you how to gather information without appearing to do so. In short, you will be a cipher."

The idea intrigued Rhoane. "It has been my experience nothing comes without a price. What do you want in return?"

Faisal stood at the windows overlooking Menurra and the harbor below. His dark brows drooped low and covered his eyes. He held a slim pipe to his lips but did not inhale the smoke that trailed from the opening like a darathi vorsi breath.

"When the Eirielle arrives, you will be her protector, Prince Rhoane, First Son of the Eleri. You must accept this challenge with the pure heart of a high priest to his goddess. You cannot falter in your belief in her, or in yourself." His words vibrated with suppressed emotion, and Rhoane quieted the questions that sprang to his lips. "I was visited by our goddess Julieta. She does not often show herself, but last night she came to me in a dream. She showed me two paths—one of destruction, one of rebirth." Faisal took a long drag from the pipe and turned to face Rhoane.

When next he spoke, the king did not speak the Summerlands vernacular, but Eleri. His voice rose several octaves and sounded nothing like Faisal, but like a young woman.

"The Darennsai cannot be raised by her mother or father. She must be taken from this world and live without knowledge of who she is. When she returns, you will guide her. Some call her the one who is and who is not. She will walk between the worlds. Only you can protect her from what is to come."

"When?" Rhoane demanded. "When will she be born?" His lingering thoughts from the previous night taunted him. *You will betray her twice, and then you will kill her.* No. *No,* he told himself—*that cannot be.* "How will I know her?"

The woman's voice once again spoke from Faisal's lips. "Ynyd Eirathnacht will know her." Faisal pointed to Rhoane's sword. "As will Claidholm Solais. Learn the song of the swords. Protect her." Her words caught, and a sob escaped.

Rhoane cocked his head and peered closer at the king. "Julieta?"

The king's body slipped back to rest upon a chair, and the form of a woman hovered in front of Rhoane. Her lush turquoise hair floated in curious spirals, and her garments were the color of waves—deepest blue to eggshell.

"Aye, it is I, First Son."

She reached a hand toward him, and he blanched at the crushed shells dotting her skin. Instead of looking like jewels, they reminded him of bruises. Her fingernails scraped along his cheek to his jaw. When his eyes sought hers, there he witnessed profound sadness, more so than he believed anyone could hope to bear. Tears stung the backs of his eyes, and he blinked quickly to dispel them.

"Do not fear for me, dearest. You will one day save us all from the torment of our past. But you must do as Faisal asks. You must become everything and nothing. A man without a kingdom, your only loyalty to the Darennsai." Grey eyes, huge against her sand-colored skin, bore into his. "Can you do this? For me? For you? For Aelinae?"

"Not for them or you," Rhoane whispered, unable to look away from the goddess. "Not even for myself. For the Darennsai."

Julieta smiled, and it brought warmth to the room. Gone was her sadness, if only for a moment. "Verdaine has chosen well." She pressed her lips to his, and thick air passed between them, coating his throat. "So you may always visit the water kingdom without fear of drowning."

She drifted away to nothingness and Rhoane was left to stare at the empty air. He touched his lips. Unanswered questions swirled in his mind.

Faisal stirred and coughed against his pipe. "What makes you moony all of a sudden?" The king pulled another drag, as if he hadn't just had his body overtaken by a goddess. "Well? Will you accept my offer?"

You will one day save us all from the torment of our past. But you must do as Faisal asks. Julieta's words teased him. He was beginning to see a pattern to the events of his life. What had Faisal said? Julieta showed him two paths. *Yes,* Rhoane thought, *our lives are always on a path. It is up to us to choose destruction or rebirth.*

Rhoane hoped he chose the right one. "When do we begin?"

"I must know you are worthy. A test first. Come with me." Faisal led him to the far courtyard, where eight men waited. Rhoane had been trained in the courtly ways of swordsmanship, but as he'd learned in Amdi's arena, street fighting had little to do with manners. Faisal, it seemed, was going to expand on his education.

Rhoane's first opponent brandished his Summerlands weapon of a short blade with two curlicues near the tip, sharp sawtooths placed between them. Rhoane drew his own sword, and the fighting commenced. It was raw and dirty, like his arena fights, but when he began to feel fatigued, another man joined the melee, then another until all eight fought against him. On and on it went until Rhoane staggered, his flailing energy barely able to hold off the men. At last, he held up his sword in defeat.

Faisal clapped slowly and circled the men who were bent over, hands on knees. Each of them wheezed as hard as Rhoane. "Well done."

Rhoane shook his head. "I lost. If this had been real, I would be dead."

"Aye, you would. But look at them. You fought for near on two bells without ever using your ShantiMari."

Rhoane's eyes widened. "The power was not allowed in Amdi's arena."

"And is life the arena, Your Highness? Will brigands and thieves care about rules?"

Of course not. Nor would they hesitate for a moment to end his life. Faisal's men were paid to let him live—others would not be. Julieta's words echoed in his mind. *You must become everything and nothing.* If he were to protect the Darennsai, he needed to be skilled as an assassin.

"Teach me," Rhoane breathed. "I will not fail you."

Faisal studied him for a moment before he nodded. "That man behind you, the one with the jeweled scimitar. Slit his throat."

"What? Why, my lord?"

"Your training begins now. You cannot think about why or if it is fair. You must be able to act without hesitation and do what must be done. That man is a spy for Lord Valterys and has been reporting your activities to his agent in Danuri. Unless you wish the Lord of the Dark and the Lady of Light to know your every move, I suggest you kill him now."

Rhoane started to turn away, but Faisal stopped him.

"Next time, I expect you to know who your enemy is without me having to point them out."

The recrimination stung. How was he to know he had enemies? He spun to face the men he'd been fighting. Several stayed hunched over, regaining their breath. The one with the jeweled scimitar rose and faced Rhoane, a challenge in his pale-grey eyes. What a fool Rhoane had been to think he didn't have enemies. Certainly there were those eager to see him dead to ensure the Darennsai's failure, or perhaps there were those who wished to know when the Darennsai was born so they could kidnap her to raise as their own. She would be powerful, more than his father, more than the empress or overlord. Gods, he'd been a fool. Running from his shame, hiding from his fear, consumed with anger.

Everything happening was beyond him yet within of him. He was an integral part of Aelinae's future; he could admit that to himself finally. He had to survive to protect the Darennsai, and to do that, he needed to take the life of any who opposed him.

Sweat slicked his palm and loosened his grip on the sword. In the arena, he'd taken many lives, and that had been to save his own. This new enemy could have killed him at any moment during the fight, but hadn't. A chilling trickle of realization crept from Rhoane's crown down his spine to settle in his gut. This man didn't want Rhoane dead. Quite the contrary. He wanted him alive to track his moves, study him, learn his weaknesses.

Rhoane glanced at the other men gathered in the courtyard. Who among them was also a spy? Did the spies work for Lliandra? Or Amdi? Or perhaps even his own father? Who could he trust?

He'd been too naïve in his dealings. That had to end. From

this moment forward, his life would be devoted to protecting the Darennsai. Until her birth, he would protect the secret of her parentage and what Julieta had told him—that she would live offworld. Until he knew who to trust, he would assume everyone was his enemy, including Faisal.

Rhoane cast a quick grin over his shoulder at the king. Yes, he would train with Faisal's men. He would learn all there was to know about being a lethal killer. He would gather information not for any monarch, but for himself. What he chose to share would be his decision, not theirs.

The men shifted uneasily, as if sensing the change in Rhoane.

He approached his target with quiet efficiency, and, before the man had a chance to speak, impaled him on his sword, twisting it savagely before he pulled it free. The other men gasped and stepped back, wary they were next. Rhoane casually took the scimitar from his victim and slit the man's throat with the razor-sharp blade. He released his grip on the weapon and it clattered to the ground. The sound echoed off the buildings in chilling, dulcet tones.

He should've been repulsed by his actions, but wasn't. Curiously, killing with purpose did not make him full of remorse, but rather it fueled him much the way his rage had. Kill or be killed. His heart pumped harder. Killing this man wasn't any easier than killing Kragor, nor did Rhoane suspect it would get any easier with each successive enemy, but it had to be done. He swallowed against the distasteful thought. There would be many more men like this one. If he, and ultimately the Darennsai, were to survive, it was the only way.

Rhoane met each man's stare, weighing their worth in his mind. "This man's loyalty was not to me or to your king. Let it be known, this is how I deal with my enemies." His heavy footfalls echoed on the tile as he stormed away.

He glanced to the cloudless sky toward Dal Tara. *Mother.* He sent the thought to the heavens. *I accept my oath and all that you asked of me.* Blood dripped from his sword to splash on his boot. His hand was stained crimson. *I will restore my lost honor in your memory. I am sorry I failed you once. It will never happen again.*

Faelara saw him and hurried over, concern etched in her features. "Rhoane, you're bleeding."

"I am not injured." He was just tired, so very tired. "But there is a man in the courtyard who is."

"What have you done?" Her amber eyes searched his. Questions lingered in their depths.

"What I must." He pressed his lips to her temple and breathed in the scent of her perfume. Right then he needed something familiar. Something comforting to soften the horror of what he'd done. What he would do in the future. "We should go swimming this afternoon."

Surprise lifted her tone. "What's happened? You're… changed."

"Aye. I am." His weariness weighed him down. "I am afraid we all will be much altered by the end of this."

He left with the cryptic words hanging between them. It was true. No one would be immune to the changes the Darennsai would bring. Good or bad, life as they knew it would cease to exist.

CHAPTER THIRTEEN

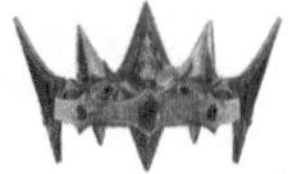

The sea churned with terrifying force. Rhoane stood at the railing, his face giving nothing away. It wouldn't do to let the crew know how much his insides roiled with the turbulent waters. Almost four seasons had passed since that first sailing from Talaith to the Summerlands and Rhoane had yet to conquer seasickness. He was certain Faelara would be mortified to know he still detested sea travel. So much had happened since that first trip. Yet in many ways, so much had stayed the same.

Faelara remained in Menurra, caring for the queen and her children. Several more had been born since he and Fae had helped the prince enter the world. Despite Rhoane's presence at the palace, he never again assisted with a birth. As Myrddin predicted, after Prince Jayved was born, the queen no longer had trouble with her pregnancies.

Rhoane only wished Empress Lliandra could say the same. Each time he visited Talaith, the rumors became louder and with increasing frequency—the empress was barren. Yet Rhoane knew this to be untrue. He never contradicted the lies; instead, he did what he could to pacify the empress, assuring her children would come in time. Even though he tried to avoid Talaith, he'd been pressed into traveling to the capital numerous times, and each occasion he entered the palace with apprehension.

Lliandra's desperation to conceive a child overrode her sense of decency and once more she began seducing Rhoane. He did his best to fend off her advances, even going so far as to beg Myrddin and Baehlon to intervene. Over the seasons, Rhoane and the giant knight became close, often traveling together when their tasks overlapped. Rhoane began to suspect the knight desired to be away from the palace in much the same way Faelara had wanted to leave Talaith.

Rhoane made it a habit to secure commissions away from Talaith expressly for Baehlon. Whether the man knew it was Rhoane who created opportunities for him to leave the Crystal Palace or not, Rhoane didn't know or care. He enjoyed Baehlon's company and, selfishly, considered it a favor to both Baehlon and Faelara.

Although he allowed Baehlon to accompany him on some jobs, Rhoane kept many of his dealings secret, even from Faisal. The king had given him a home when he was lost. He was kind and generous, and allowed Rhoane space to adapt and learn, but there were some things Rhoane must do that no one ever need know about. After Julieta's visit in Faisal's room all those seasons ago, Rhoane had become focused on one thing—protecting the Darennsai. When the time came and she was ready to claim her place in Aelinae's history, Rhoane would be there to guide and protect, just as Julieta had commanded of him.

To do so, there were certain events he must ensure take place, like the nasty business that brought him to the west on this godforsaken ship. From the corner of his eye, Rhoane caught the flounce of a rather large black feather. Internally he groaned and outwardly turned to greet the captain. Ivyn was a man Rhoane knew from previous voyages and, despite his egregious attire, admired.

This was the trickiest part of his journey and he needed to be assured everything would go to plan. They'd been at sea for a fort-night, traveling by night, with little to light their way. But the captain had put his faith in Rhoane, and thus far, he hadn't led them astray. Now, though, he had to find a cove where they could drop anchor without being seen. Everything depended on Rhoane being untraceable.

"Your Highness." The captain flounced into a bow and Rhoane winced. "We are nearing our terminus. Have you any last instructions for my crew?"

Rhoane hadn't told the man who he was, nor did he give his real name. Yet Ivyn insisted on calling him "Your Highness" as a mocking gesture, and each time he did, Rhoane wanted to stab a dagger in the man's throat.

"Just do as we discussed. Sail in as quietly as possible and drop anchor. I will alight from your ship without delay and you may continue your voyage north."

"Still not going to tell me why you want to be let off in the middle of nowhere?"

Rhoane turned his gaze fully to the man. "No."

"Righto. You there!" Ivyn called to a deckhand and blasted him with orders before leaving Rhoane alone at the railing.

When they reached the cove, Rhoane scanned the clifftops and beach, making certain no one saw them. Satisfied, he threw his leg over the railing and lowered himself into the waiting dinghy. They rowed to shore and only Rhoane exited the little boat. Without turning back, he headed across the beach toward the cliffs and began the treacherous business of scaling the steep slope, his only light the scant cast of the half moon.

By the time he reached the top, the ship was far enough at sea he could barely make out the emblem on the sails. At least the captain was a man of his word. Rhoane had been half afraid the fool would stick around just to see what Rhoane did next.

What he needed to do, no one could know about. It came

with the business of being the beloved of the Darennsai. As distasteful as it was, there was no other way.

Rhoane swallowed against the pit that formed in his throat. Even now, after several seasons of training with Faisal's men, there were things that turned his stomach and bit at his conscience. With each new task, as he likened them, he learned to shut off his emotions and do the job as cleanly—without remorse—as possible. But this task he knew would be difficult to forget.

He squinted at the horizon, determining how much time he had before full sunrise. Less than one bell. The nearest town was a half days' walk, but Rhoane wanted to spend as little time there as possible. The fewer people who saw him, the less energy expended on blending in. He made it a rule to not use Shanti-Mari on his tasks. To do so might draw the wrong sort of attention to himself and if he were to truly be a cipher, attention wasn't what he required. Not wanting to arrive too soon, he slowed his pace and headed northeast.

Valterys's kingdom was a prosperous one with well-maintained roads and flourishing market towns, which served Rhoane well. He arrived at his destination shortly before sundown and was able to not only secure a mount, but also a room in a modest inn. As he sat alone at his table, he eavesdropped on the townsfolk, marking anything that sounded important. What he discovered was the overlord ruled not as a tyrant, but as a compassionate leader who listened to his subjects' concerns with fairness.

To hear the townsfolk speak of Valterys in such glowing terms both relieved and irritated Rhoane. For not only did they admire their overlord, they adored his wife as well. In fact, with their son Zakael entering his ninth season, many in the common room voiced their hopes for a brother or sister for the heir.

Rhoane ate in silence, knowing Zakael would indeed have a sister, but not anytime soon. As part of his quest to become the Darennsai's protector, he'd read as many oracles and prophecies as he could find. What he came to believe was exactly as Julieta predicted—that the Darennsai could only be conceived by the Lady of Light and the Lord of the Dark. The anomaly, as some called the Darennsai, would be a fusion of the three strains of ShantiMari—Light, Dark, and Eleri. An aberration some called her, but Rhoane chose to believe that through her embodiment of all three strands of ShantiMari, she would succeed in balancing Aelinae where others would fail. Their world existed as a delicate nucleus to not only the stars and terrarae, but everything beyond what they could see.

Lliandra's high priest Brandt had shown Rhoane images of stars past their familiar constellations in the night sky and Julieta had told Rhoane the Darennsai would walk between worlds. Few on Aelinae understood the relationship this world had with others, but Rhoane and Brandt suspected the Darennsai was the key to maintaining peace not only on Aelinae, but beyond the stars as well.

The next morning, Rhoane left the town before most of the residents had stirred from their beds. Caer Idris was a day's ride north. The sooner he completed this task, the better. The nag he'd bought in town was serviceable for his needs, but chaffed at Rhoane's impatience. He missed his stallion Luc, who waited for him in Danuri, along with Claidholm Solais and his Eleri clothing. For this mission, he'd disguised himself as a down on his luck courtier from one of the smaller regions of Danuri. He wore a wig to hide his short locks and slightly tipped ears, and clothed himself in several seasons' past finery of a velvet jacket, lightweight traveling cloak, and wide, full legged trousers. His soft boots were worn and scuffed. In all, he did his best to appear like a man who'd once been important, but had yet to fully embrace the concept he no longer was.

On the road to Caer Idris, Rhoane met several fellow travelers, all of whom had stories to tell of why they traveled to the capital and what they hoped to find there. To each he listened and offered his story of seeking an audience with the Great Lord. Many of his companions offered tips on what to say, who to ask, all of which Rhoane stored for later. This task required him to make his presence known at the castle, something which sat uncomfortably with him. He much preferred clean tasks, without any witnesses, and certainly not in public. But this necessary business had to be carried out in front of the court of Caer Idris. The trick was to make it seem natural so no one could ever be implicated, least of all, Rhoane.

By the time the city gates loomed before him, Rhoane had a working plan of how best to execute his task. At the huge gates to the castle, he presented the forged letter he carried imploring the overlord Valterys to give this worthy courtier a bed for the night. It wasn't uncommon for foreign nobility and court attendees to seek shelter from a neighboring lord, and from what Rhoane had learned, Valterys rarely turned travelers away.

The guard at the gate read his letter and passed it to another man, who ran from the gate to the castle proper. Rhoane waited on his horse, a bored expression cemented into place. When the lad returned a quarter bell later, Rhoane was instructed to leave his horse with the stable boys and to follow the page. After seeing to his nag, he did as instructed and silently followed the page into the vast castle.

Whereas the Crystal Palace was filled with light from the massive glass walls, Caer Idris's great stone corridors were suffocating. Large torches lit the damp spaces, giving off heat for a second or two as they passed. After a short distance, they turned a corner and entered the great hall. Chandeliers hung from the ceiling with hundreds of candles providing light. Despite the rough stone walls, the room had the sense of lightness and joy.

Musicians played in one corner with several tables set at inconsistent intervals, providing places where courtiers could sit and talk or play games. Rhoane took in the entirety of the room with a quick glance. Laughter bubbled up from many different conversations, but one in particular caught his attention. Troyanna Djeba, consort to the Overlord of the West, mother to Zakael, sat with a group of women in the center of the room. Hair like a raven's and shimmering olive skin complemented the ruby-colored dress she wore. She was a gem amid seashells.

The page made a line straight for Troyanna, and Rhoane checked that his posture was one of obsequiousness. He tilted his head lower, his shoulders forward a touch. After the page introduced him, Rhoane bowed low, nearly to the floor.

"My lady, it is an honor to make your acquaintance." He rolled his hand in an obscene flourish, a wide smile stretching his lips.

"You are from Danuri?" A slight Danurian accent echoed in her speech.

"Yes, from Calzean."

"Oh." Her voice dropped. Disappointment hung on that one syllable. "I had hoped you came from closer to home. I'm afraid I never had the pleasure of visiting Calzean. Who is the lord there?"

Rhoane supplied the answer, and several more to her challenging questions. He'd been through this dance many times and knew to give enough information he appeared genuine, without giving more than could be verified. Once she was satisfied, Rhoane was led to a small room on the first floor. Little more than servant's quarters, but he didn't care about the size of his room or where it was located. He'd come for a single purpose and would only be there a few nights.

After freshening up from his travels, he changed into more suitable court attire and roamed the castle. The chances of running into someone from the Crystal Palace were thin, but Rhoane was alert to danger all the same. He'd done his best to physically alter his appearance, but unless he used his power to mask his identity, there was only so much clothing and a wig could do. The rest had to come from his countenance and speech.

He walked with a slight stiffness, the gait of a man who knew he'd once been important, and hated to find himself begging for a bed. The consort's questions weren't alarming in the least, but to the man Rhoane pretended to be, they were insulting, yet had to be endured.

He strolled affecting and appearance of the inner affliction the interview had caused. Self-pity, a bit of pride (albeit damaged), and gratitude he'd not been thrown out on the street. The gardens provided him with a chance to collect his thoughts. Several courtiers milled about, some seated on benches, others walking along the pebbled paths of the formal garden. Rhoane controlled his steps, not stepping too lightly nor too hard upon the ground. He didn't want to make his presence known and yet needed to be seen. It was a delicate balance.

At the end of the garden, he turned a corner and saw a lone tree silhouetted against the sky. It sat upon a cliff top with nothing near or around it for several paces. Intrigued, he headed toward the tree, but the closer he came, the sicker he felt. Nausea toiled in his throat. The odd tree had no leaves, only a black trunk and branches. What looked like thorns dotted the bark from the soil to the tips of each branch. The Eleri knew every tree, flower, and grass on Aelinae, but this—thing—had him perplexed.

"I hate that thing," a voice said behind him.

Rhoane schooled his expression into one of distaste before turning around to face his visitor. A young man of perhaps forty seasons stared past Rhoane to the black tree.

"I have never seen one of its kind. Do you know what it is called?"

"A runyon tree. No one can go near it but Valterys and his son. It sickens me."

"Me as well." Rhoane turned from the man and headed toward the gardens. Beyond them, the sea stretched as far as the eye could see. "With such beauty, why mar the landscape with that?"

The man shook his head. "I wish I knew. Even the consort hates it, but the overlord is adamant it stays." Then, remembering his manners, the young man bent at the waist in an acceptable bow. "I'm Anje. Valterys is my cousin." His eyes rolled up and he shrugged. "I might not like his decorating style, but it's his castle —he makes the rules."

Rhoane introduced himself, using the fake name and title. They walked on, chatting about the flowers and shrubs in the garden, but Rhoane couldn't dislodge the unsettling feeling the runyon tree brought on. Something wasn't right with it, but he couldn't say what.

For two days, Rhoane stayed close to the castle grounds, sometimes accompanying Duke Anje on walks, other times sitting quietly in the great hall and observing. As luck would have it, Valterys and his son were away from the castle on business, which left Rhoane free to accomplish his task and not have to face the Lord of the Dark.

His third night at Caer Idris was filled with thunderstorms that shook the castle windows and threatened to topple trees. Rhoane waited until the servants went to bed before he left his room and silently made his way to the consort's sleeping quarters. Like many noble women, she slept with several of her ladies-in-waiting, which was excellent for Rhoane's plan.

He crept between them to the bed where Troyanna lay, her dark hair plaited and face peaceful. She bore the look of one without a care in the world, and why should she not? Her husband was the most powerful man in the west, and she'd given him an heir. Rhoane brushed her thoughts and confirmed that she was not with child at present. He'd heard too many rumors to trust that she might yet be pregnant. Fortunately, although she dreamed of more children, she'd not yet conceived a second child from Valterys.

Rhoane let out a small sigh of relief. It was the only sticking point to his plan—if Troyanna were with child, he would have to wait. He was an assassin, yes, but he refused to murder innocent children.

One of the women sleeping with Troyanna snuffled and shifted, her face tilted toward her lady's. Rhoane placed her hand over the consort's and sent his power through her. She would act as a conductor in case Valterys had an accomplished mage who could sense the use of ShantiMari. By using the lady-in-waiting as a go-between, any power detected would be hers.

Very gently, Rhoane coaxed the woman's power into Troyanna, with suggestions to the consort's heart to stop beating. Her death had to appear natural. There could be no questions asked, and no suspicion placed on him or anyone else at court. Valterys must mourn his consort and in time look for another lover to warm his bed. If he suspected murder, it would derail him from Lliandra's path.

Unfortunately for Troyanna, her being alive prevented the birth of the Darennsai. The longer she stayed with Valterys, and the more children she provided him, the harder it would be for the Lord of the Dark to mate with the Lady of Light.

Rhoane had reasoned it all out in his mind several times, but still the act did not ease his conscience or heart.

Troyanna moaned and tossed with the influx of power, but Rhoane sent a thought that she should be at peace. He willed calm to her mind while continuing to slow her heartbeat. After several long moments, her face went slack and her breathing stopped.

It was done.

Let his goddess condemn him, but he'd done what he must for the Darennsai.

CHAPTER FOURTEEN

Faelara inhaled the heady scent of spice, a grin on her lips. She'd been surprised by Lliandra's agreement to allow Summerlands merchants to sell their goods in Talaith, but grateful all the same. She'd heard rumors the empress liked the idea so much she'd opened trade routes to Danuri, as well. Faelara looked forward to seeing the changes for herself when she returned to Talaith.

Her stomach pinched at the thought. For four seasons she'd stayed in the Summerlands, finding one excuse after another not to return home. Baehlon had married Micah three seasons past, but she'd heard he spent much of his time away from the palace. That gave her little comfort. He could've said no to the empress. He could've fought for Faelara.

And she could've been honest with him and told him how she felt.

They were both to blame, but that didn't mean she had to live under Lliandra's roof and watch the newlyweds ogle each other. Gods forbid what she'd do when Micah became pregnant, and eventually she would. That was, after all, Lliandra's reason for putting the pair together. For the empress, marriage rarely meant love, but was always for political advantage. Well-honed anger simmered in her veins. The empress ruled with absolute obedience. Anyone who disagreed with her either found themselves exiled from the east, or imprisoned, or worse. Faelara had no intention of ever getting on her bad side, which meant she probably should never return to Talaith. Her anger at her sovereign could be construed as treason.

As far as she was concerned, the only treasonous person was Baehlon. Well, and possibly Micah, and certainly the empress herself. After all, Micah and Baehlon wouldn't have been married if not for Lliandra's command. The circular logic twisted itself through her thoughts on a familiar circuit. Each time she caught herself in the torturous trap, she'd think of Jayved and the queen. Her sanctuary. Her salvation.

A shadow caught her attention, and she glanced to her left. A swath of chestnut hair caught in the sun, and she squinted into the darkened alcove. Seeing nothing, she shook her head. For several days, she'd had the feeling she was being watched, that someone spied on her whenever she strolled the market or when she took Prince Jayved to the private cove, where she taught him to swim. He was a stocky boy with a healthy laugh and the sweetest black curls. Faelara had quite lost her heart to the child. If she were honest with herself, she'd admit it was the prince who had saved her from absolute heartache.

Queen Prateeni continued to care for her firstborn, but she allowed Faelara unprecedented access to him, as if sensing her need to bond with another. She and the queen had grown close in the time Faelara had been in the Summerlands. Especially with Rhoane's extended trips to gods knew where. He often disappeared for several moonturns at a time. At first, she worried about him constantly—he was still little more than a boy and innocent about the world—but each time he returned, she saw in him a maturity he'd not possessed before.

King Faisal's training was harsh and often caused Rhoane

distress, but he kept his feelings closely guarded. On the rare occasions he'd confessed to her his anguish, she'd been shocked to learn the extent of his training. The Summerlands king was turning Rhoane into more than a spy or an assassin, and Faelara wasn't sure she liked it one bit.

But Faisal was determined to see Rhoane prepared for what was to come. Although, no one knew when or what would happen. His approach was to be ready for anything at any time. Simple logic, Faelara had to admit, but upsetting all the same.

Another movement caught her eye, and she glared at the shadows. Either she was losing her mind, or someone *was* following her.

A figure hovered to her left, much too close, and Faelara suppressed a cry. She stepped aside, but a hand caught her waist and pulled her against a solid torso.

"Unhand me this instant, you brute!" She swiveled to face the menace and immediately softened. "Rhoane. What in Ohlin's name are you doing?"

"I have told you to be more cautious, Faelara. If I wished you harm, you would be dead by now."

"I'm shopping. How much harm could befall me in a crowded marketplace?" She kept her tone casual, but his words hit true. If she'd had the prince with her, she'd have left them both open to being kidnapped. Rhoane had indeed taught her better than that.

He picked up a pot and inhaled deeply. "Hanan has the finest spices of all Aelinae. But do not tell my sister I said so. She believes hers are superior." He winked at her and called the merchant over. After he gave his order, he turned back to her. "How have you been, Faelara?"

This time he'd been gone half a season, the longest trip yet. From his pale skin, she assumed he'd been somewhere on the mainland. "To be honest, I've missed you. And I'm beginning to miss Talaith, as well."

"Then I bring you good news, I hope." His eyes searched hers, and a tremble of fear started at her scalp. "Empress Lliandra is with child. She wishes for you to return at once to help deliver the baby." A cloud passed over his eyes, turning them a darker shade of green.

"What aren't you telling me?"

A grin broke his solemn features. "You know me too well, my friend. Lliandra expects this child to be the One, but she will be disappointed. This is not the Eirielle, but a boy child conceived from a minor noble."

"How do you know?" Rhoane had ways of knowing things Faelara had long since stopped trying to uncover, yet the question always came.

"I just do." Again, the sly grin.

Hanan returned with Rhoane's spices and fawned over Faelara for several minutes. Each week, she visited him to get the ingredients needed for her tea.

"What can I get you today? The usual?"

Faelara gripped his hand, not wanting to say the words. "I'm afraid I'll need more this week. It seems we'll be leaving soon, and I don't know when I'll return."

Hanan's face fell. "I'm sorry to hear it, my lady. Tabul!" He called his eldest son over to fetch Faelara's goods.

She gave him a longer list than usual and promised to return in a little while to collect the goods. Her hand slid comfortably into the crook of Rhoane's arm. They strolled the market, purchased several fruits, and chatted about his travels (as much as he was willing to share) and the events at the palace.

"What will you do once we're in Talaith?" Faelara asked. "Certainly Faisal won't continue to send you on mysterious missions."

Rhoane chuckled good-naturedly. "The king has been more than kind to me. If he has need of me, I will help, but while we are in Talaith, I will make it my duty to learn all I can about

Lliandra's court. With you gone, she was reluctant to allow me to stay for longer than a few days at most." He leaned in and whispered conspiratorially, "I do not think she likes me overmuch. I refuse to share her bed, and this vexes her."

Laughter bubbled up from Faelara's sternum, which lifted her mood. "I can only imagine. She's not accustomed to men telling her no."

Rhoane carried their purchases as they trundled up the steep road to the palace where the king and queen waited for them. In Faisal's hands was Lliandra's royal summons. Tears streaked both their faces, and Faelara was taken aback that they would miss her as much as she would miss them.

"You will see your father again," Faisal told her as he hugged her to within an inch of her life.

She'd missed her father terribly. Seeing him would bring her great comfort. In his absence, Faisal had provided her with wise council and she looked on him as a foster father. It would not be easy to leave the monarchs or their children, but it was time.

They sailed for Talaith two days later. When they rounded the rocky coast and saw Talaith's harbor, Faelara burst into tears, mortifying the few sailors who stood nearby. She hadn't realized how much she'd missed home.

Rhoane put a protective arm around her shoulder, and she sank into him, burying her face and her tears. In the quiet moments of her day, she accepted the brutal truth that she'd run away to the Summerlands and now she'd have to face her fears and her hopes. It wasn't enough to simply return. She had to face her future and to do so, she needed to let go of her past. A mantra played on repeat in her mind—to accept her life whatever it encompassed. A flutter of uncertainty slowed her thoughts. It was one thing to tell herself she had to move on, but she knew seeing Baehlon would be difficult. Despite everything, her feelings for him hadn't changed.

By the time they were to unload, she'd composed herself enough to disembark with the dignity of a lady.

Not much had changed in the four seasons of her absence. Lliandra was even more demanding now that she was with child. The poor father, a minor noble who lived on the coast near Gaarendahl, hovered over the empress to the point of distraction. She was eight moonturns along and big enough to suspect twins, but Faelara sensed only one child in her womb. A male, as Rhoane had predicted.

Which meant after his birth, he'd be sent to live with his father, with a seasonly stipend and no communication with his mother.

Except the child would first have to prove he wasn't the Eirielle. Despite Rhoane's insistence the one of prophecy would be female, Lliandra refused to trust his opinion.

On the night of the child's birth, the goddess Nadra appeared with the sword Ohlin had made for their daughter Daknys. Two dragons flanked the hilt, and a ruby sparkled upon the pommel. Those in the room gasped when they saw it, for most believed the fabled sword had been lost.

"Bring him to me," Nadra commanded Faelara and she gently removed the newborn from his mother's arms.

Regardless of her insistence she would reject a male, the moment he was born Lliandra's face glowed with pride. She took him from the midwife and held him close to her breast. Faelara separated mother and son with a slice of guilt. Sorrow etched across Lliandra's features when the child left her embrace and a moment later, a veil of cool indifference fell into place.

When the newborn's palm was placed upon the pommel, he screamed as if burned. Nadra shook her head. "I am sorry, Lliandra, he is not the One." She handed the baby to Faelara and disappeared with the sword.

Faelara snuggled the babe to her breast and made cooing noises to settle his cries. The poor thing didn't know what was happening and had no idea the significance of the proceedings. He was innocent and should be loved. It pained her to know he'd be cast aside simply because of his gender.

Those gathered breathed a sigh of relief, but the empress remained unaffected. Faelara reluctantly handed the child to the father, and they were both whisked away. A maw of emptiness engulfed Faelara and she blinked back tears. The nobles and midwives shifted uneasily, unsure what to do next. There was no child to coddle, no care to give, except to the empress and she refused anyone touching her.

If they expected the empress to show anguish, they were to be disappointed. After a moment of reflection, Lliandra had beamed. "We should not mourn the loss of the child," she instructed those gathered in her room, "but celebrate the fact I am not barren."

Faelara didn't care that Lliandra had stolen her words. Because that night, the court needed joy to spring forth from a devastating situation and Lliandra provided just that. Faelara's repressed anger at her sovereign began to thaw. Her reticence at seeing Baehlon also diminished. If she were to live at the Crystal Palace, she would have to see him, and Micah. Putting her feelings aside would be best. Hard as it would be—she would shove her love to the far reaches of her spirit where it wouldn't interfere in their lives.

Faelara tore her gaze away from the empress to the corner of the room where Baehlon stood with the other men. A discreet screen hid Lliandra from them, but where Faelara stood, she could see him clearly. He stood beside Rhoane, on their faces looks of twin concern. Yet Baehlon did not look to the other side of the room where Lliandra was being healed as Rhoane did—he stared directly at her.

Her heart did a somersault and she swallowed hard. Her feelings for the knight had not lessened in her time away. If she were to succeed at court, and as one of Lliandra's ladies-in-waiting, she would have to control her emotions. It wouldn't do to have the entire palace gossiping about her and Sir Baehlon. She met his stare and smiled, a terse, polite, close-lipped affair that she hoped signaled to him that she held him in no higher regard than any other man. After a moment, he turned away and strode from the room. Faelara let out a tortured sigh and returned to her empress.

"I do not envy you," a soft voice said near her and Faelara's fragile heart sank. "It can't have been easy to lose him and then to come back to a joyous affair that ended like this."

"Thank you, Micah, for your concern. It wasn't as hard as I'd thought." The lie slid easily off her tongue.

Baehlon's wife put a hand on Faelara's. "I know it's an imposition, but I would like to still be friends if at all possible." Her gaze flicked toward the empress. "We all do what we must, and I hope that won't interfere with the sisterhood we once shared."

What was Micah saying? She didn't love Baehlon? Faelara's head spun with the knowledge. She'd assumed Micah would be happy for the arrangement.

"I would like that. I have missed your company these long seasons that I was away." It was true. With a shock, Faelara realized she'd been holding so much contempt for Baehlon she'd all but forgotten how close she and Micah once were.

Her heart felt lighter than it had in ages and she went about her tasks with a sense of purpose and hope for the future. Hers, Baehlon's, the empress's. For the first time in a long while, she looked forward to her days at the palace.

CHAPTER FIFTEEN

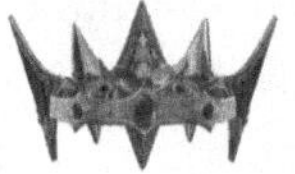

A fortnight after Lliandra gave birth, Valterys, Overlord of the West, Lord of the Dark, arrived for a visit. The moment he entered Lliandra's lavish sitting room, Faelara knew there was something special about this man. Her empress acted contrary to her usually controlled self, giggling too much and fidgeting with her jewels constantly.

The overlord brought his son Zakael, a clever lad with striking grey eyes and a shock of black hair. With him, too, came his cousin, Duke Anje. If Lliandra acted childishly infatuated with the overlord, her sister Gwyneira acted the exact opposite. Her attraction to the duke was almost contrite.

The visitors from the west stayed two moonturns at the Crystal Palace and each day in the overlord's company, Lliandra grew stronger and Faelara surreptitiously facilitated as many impromptu meetings of the pair as she could. With Rhoane's, and sometimes Myrddin's, help, she was able to secure the empress's quarters, allowing the royal pair privacy. Always under the guise of discussing diplomatic relations between the east and west.

The friendship Lliandra and Valterys formed over that

moonturn would be good for all of Aelinae. Faelara was only doing her civic duty. If a romance blossomed from her efforts, who was she to deny her empress happiness? Despite her best efforts, the overlord mourned the loss of his wife, who had taken ill and died only a short time before Faelara had returned to Talaith.

When it was time for the overlord and his son to leave, the duke sought a formal meeting with Lliandra, and Faelara's heart sank. For all her contriving with Valterys, she feared Lliandra had fallen in love with the duke. At the appointed time of their meeting, she made up an excuse to be in Lliandra's rooms.

Her heart stopped in her throat when Anje entered, looking as nervous as a man going to the gallows. He held his cap in hand, wringing it between his fingers.

Lliandra reclined on a sofa, her long blonde curls cascading over her barely concealed breasts. Faelara's heart beat harder; her breath came in shallow pulls. The empress was in her finest form, wearing her most alluring gown, her most precious gems dotting her hair, throat, and wrists. Duke Anje wouldn't stand a chance against Lliandra.

The duke bowed, clearing his throat as he did. "Your Majesty, I've come here today to ask your permission to stay on at the Crystal Palace when my cousin departs on the morrow."

Faelara kept to the background as much as possible, but she had to lean forward to hear the duke, he spoke so low. When the words registered, an anxious pit formed in her stomach. All that work, for nothing. Anje was not meant for Lliandra. Sure, he would make a fine lover, and possibly could be the father of the Eirielle, but Faelara had seen the way he looked at Princess Gwyneira. Did she have it so wrong? Had Anje been playing them false all along? She eased a step closer, keeping close to the wall. On the other side of the room, Myrddin entered, with Baehlon close behind. When they saw Faelara, their expressions turned curious, then they as a pair noticed the duke and empress in her sitting room. Understanding dawned and they joined her without making a sound.

"The duke wishes to ask Lliandra something," Faelara whispered an explanation.

Myrddin nodded and tugged at his beard. Baehlon's expression didn't change. He also didn't turn toward the empress as the mage did. He kept his gaze on her.

Unsettled by their presence, Faelara smoothed her skirts and did her best to ignore them both. Anje was speaking again and she didn't want to miss what was said.

"…am in love and wish to ask for permission to marry."

"No," Fae gasped and put a hand over her mouth. Myrddin scowled in her direction with a finger over his lips. Baehlon, as always, remained impassive.

"And is my sister in love with you, Duke Anje?" From Lliandra's tone, it was clear she knew Gwyn's position on the situation. Faelara let out a deep sigh and felt her heartbeat return to normal.

"I believe so, yes. If you grant me permission to stay, we will know within a moonturn or two if she is, and if so, I would like to marry her. If not, then I will return to the west and never bother you again."

Oh, no. The duke had allowed an opening for the empress to snag him if she chose.

Lliandra leaned forward until her cleavage was close enough for the duke to touch. "What if she denies you and some other woman in the palace wants you for her own? Would you be amenable to staying on for her sake?"

Anje cleared his throat and looked the empress in the eye. "No, Your Majesty, I would not. If Princess Gwyneira denies me, I'm afraid my heart would be broken and no other woman could heal such a wound."

Faelara silently cheered the man.

Lliandra leaned back, settling herself into the cushions.

"You'd be surprised how easily the heart is mended with a warm body curled against your own."

The wording Lliandra chose, and the sly smile on her lips, gave Faelara hope. Perhaps the overlord and the empress had bonded in their shared grief. Hope once again bloomed in her heart.

"Do you grant me permission to stay and court your sister?"

"Yes, of course. I might be the empress of Talaith, Your Grace, but I am still a woman. Anyone with half a sight can see Gwyneira's beside herself in love with you and I can deny my sister nothing."

It was done. Duke Anje was spoken for and with any luck, Lliandra would soon be smitten with another highborn noble and the Eirielle conceived. Faelara knew her choice, but it was ultimately Lliandra's prerogative who she slept with. First, she had a wedding to help plan. Gwyneira was like a sister to Faelara, and she would do everything in her power to guarantee a perfect day for the princess.

As promised, Anje and Gwyneira were married the following summer, on a glorious day with little heat and no surprise showers. The entire palace was alive with excitement for the couple and it soon had even more reason to celebrate when the princess announced she was pregnant. A son was born nine moonturns later. Unlike male children born to the empress, this son was allowed to stay at the palace to be raised by his jubilant parents.

In time, Faelara saw the pain the little boy caused the empress and it wasn't long after his birth she made the duke protector of Paderau and sent her sister to live with him in the expansive palace there. Faelara wept with Gwyneira the day of their parting and as they passed through the gates, a hole was left in Fae's heart. Lliandra could be selfish and cruel when she wished and some of that old anger ran through Faelara's veins once again.

Once the court quieted down after the departure of Gwyn's family, Lliandra began in earnest her search for the father of her next child. It didn't take long until she found a handsome noble of high regard, and he dutifully gave Lliandra a child. Once again the palace halls were full of excited chatter as the court prepared for the birth.

Princess Marissa was born on a clear morning during Wintertide. Her rosy cheeks warmed the hearts of all those present for her birth. Lliandra beamed to finally have an heir. When Nadra appeared with the sword and Marissa screamed when her palm was placed upon the pommel, Lliandra hid her disappointment behind a tight smile. Faelara knew the empress had been convinced this child would be the One. Lliandra had told her as much on too many occasions.

Those in Talaith cared little that Marissa wasn't the Eirielle. They had an heir to the Light Throne and that alone was cause for celebration. The festivities lasted for well over a week, with music and feasts and balls, all for the little princess who was too young to enjoy any of it. As heir, Marissa was guarded night and day. As soon as she began to speak, the best tutors were found for her, and the most skilled mages taught her how to weave her ShantiMari. Esna, Marissa's father, enjoyed a comfortable life at the Crystal Palace. In addition to providing the empress with a daughter, he fathered a son with Lliandra and suffered through two miscarriages with her.

Throughout all of Lliandra's heartache and joy, Faelara stayed true to her empress. She assisted in the births of the heir and her brother, as well as eased Lliandra's pain through the two tragedies. Without the support of her father, Faelara might have left the Crystal Palace to stay with Gwyneira in Paderau, but Brandt had convinced her the empress needed her and, after all the ups and downs of court life, Faelara was glad she'd listened to him.

Lliandra did indeed need her, but she needed to forgive Baehlon and herself and the only way she was able to do so was to push through the discomfort. Seeing Baehlon still made her heart flutter, but she'd finally been able to put her feelings aside and be friends with him and his wife, Micah. Fortunately for Fae, the knight often spent long periods away from the palace. Even Rhoane continued his disappearing act. Sometimes Faelara suspected the pair went off together, but she neither asked after their mysterious trips, nor did they offer information. She did, however, keep track of them through her father and sometimes Myrddin.

Both the high priest and the mage could be cagey with their answers, but that didn't stop Fae from asking them. It almost became a game with the trio. One brilliant Frost End day, they were sitting in the conservatory, quietly reading, when Faelara decided to prod them for information about Rhoane's latest quest. She sipped her tea and kept her gaze firmly on a spot outside the windows where Gwyneira's rose bushes were just starting to bud.

"Do you think Rhoane will return by summer? I should like to visit the duke and duchess in Paderau and I was hoping he could escort me."

"If you'd like to see Gwyn, I could take you," Brandt offered.

"I've been meaning to travel that way myself," Myrddin seconded.

"You two are sweet, but really, I wanted to see if Rhoane would be amenable to taking me to Ulla. He promised me ages ago he would." It was a bold lie, but she wanted to see her father's and Myrddin's expressions.

They did not disappoint.

"You would do well to stay far from Ulla. When Rhoane returns, I shall have a word with him. What's he thinking, making that promise to you?"

"Calm down, Father. They do have women in Ulla, you know. They aren't complete savages."

Myrddin sipped his tea and stared over the rim of his cup. "If you'd truly like to visit Ulla, I might be able to arrange it. Be warned, Amdi, Laird of the Clans, does not suffer anyone trespassing on his lands, nor is he known for his generosity."

Faelara recalled the stories Rhoane once shared of his time in Ulla. "Are you friends with the laird?"

"Friends? Not quite. We respect each other." Myrddin stroked his beard, his eyes far away in thought. "No, not friends." He snapped his attention to Faelara. "I think it would be best if you didn't travel to Ulla. There has been unrest there of late and you would not be safe. In my company, or Rhoane's."

Faelara opened her mouth to argue, but her father's quick shake of his head silenced her. Nothing more was said about Ulla. Not only had she not discovered where Rhoane and Baehlon were, she'd successfully prevented any future attempts to visit the desert kingdom. For certainly her father or Myrddin would tell Rhoane about their discussion and he would refuse to take her.

Faelara did travel to Paderau to see Gwyneira and the duke with Brandt as her companion. They stayed a full moonturn in the palace and by the end of their visit, Faelara promised to return as often as she could. The atmosphere in Paderau was relaxed and happy. Anyone could see how in love the duke and duchess were, and they doted on their son. It was as Fae had hoped the Crystal Palace would be with Lliandra's children running around, but the two palaces were complete opposites. For the empress, her heir was all that mattered. The poor little prince was tolerated, but not well loved by his mother.

Faelara kept her promise and visited Paderau as often as Lliandra would allow. Her friendship with Gwyneira deepened with each visit until it was almost impossible for Faelara to leave. But the empress demanded her presence and each time Fae said goodbye to Gwyn and Anje, she feared it would be the last time. She knew Lliandra could be cold and punished those she thought happier than herself. One day, that would very likely be Faelara.

Despite Lliandra's mercurial moods, the court lived in relative calm until the Crown Princess was five seasons old and Marissa's father Esna was caught trying to poison the empress. The gossip around the palace went into a tizzy when the plot was uncovered. Some whispered he was innocent, that this was a device Lliandra had concocted to be rid of him; others said Esna had tried several times to murder the empress. Faelara, like many of the courtiers, heard the news with shocked dismay. If Lliandra wished to be rid of Esna, all she had to do was relieve him of duty, but Marissa's father had gained favor at court. There were many who liked the brash noble, and he was rumored to have more than enough coin to raise an army if he wished. Faelara suspected it was those two reasons that had kept him in Lliandra's favor for so long.

Esna's execution was swift and never publicly spoken of by Lliandra afterward. The young prince, three at the time of his father's death, was stripped of his titles and given to Esna's sister to raise. Both were banished from Lliandra's court.

Marissa barely acknowledged her father's death or her brother's absence. Only once did Faelara see the princess weep for her father. They were in Lliandra's sitting room when Faelara saw tears rolling softly down the girl's cheeks.

Instinctively, she went to cuddle the child. "You poor lamb. There now, there, there."

"Do not give in to her blubbering, Faelara," Lliandra said. "Marissa, dry your eyes and come here."

Marissa squirmed out of Faelara's embrace and went to her mother.

"You understand why Esna was punished, yes?" Marissa nodded slowly, her eyes damp and unfocused. "He was a traitor and those who wish harm to you or I must be dealt with. You would do well to remember this. As my heir, and someday the Lady of Light, there will be many who would try to kill you or worse. Never let them see your tears. Always show strength. If you show weakness, they will be merciless in their attack. You must always strike first. Do you promise you will remember?"

"Yes, Mama."

Lliandra's eyes narrowed and a hiss escaped her lips.

"Yes, Your Majesty. I will remember."

"Your throne is all that matters, Marissa." She clucked the princess on her chin. "You and I must always take care of each other. Yes?"

Marissa nodded solemnly and Faelara looked away. She couldn't bear to see the young girl stripped of her childhood.

The palace became a place of tension after Esna's beheading. The empress continued to rule, but a cloud had descended over her. She had her heir, and refused to take anyone to her bed. Of the Eirielle, she refused to entertain any discussions.

Late that summer, the overlord and his son visited again. Faelara watched the sun return to her empress's heart, and she knew. As she'd hoped, this was the man who would fulfill the prophecy. She recalled a conversation she'd had with Rhoane in a crowded Summerlands marketplace many seasons earlier and wondered whether he'd always known it would be Valterys.

She glanced to where Rhoane leaned casually against the wall, home from whatever dire situation had called him away, at ease in the palace now that Lliandra no longer pursued him. He caught her eye and grinned—a sloppy, roguish grin she suspected had broken more than one woman's heart. He'd grown into a fine man over the course of their friendship.

What? The gentle thought brushed her mind.

You knew, didn't you? She cast a quick glance at Valterys, who was making a show of kissing Lliandra's fingers.

Rhoane shrugged in answer.

Infuriating man!

Zakael, Valterys's son, now twenty seasons and even more handsome, stood to the side, looking bored at the antics of his lovesick father. Yes, Faelara realized, Valterys was equally attracted to Lliandra.

Like an orphaned puppy, Marissa followed Zakael every-where. He tolerated her presence, but only just. She was a child and he on the cusp of adulthood. He kept his visits short, but each time he came to Talaith, the princess was drawn to him like fleas to a mongrel.

For ten seasons, Valterys courted Lliandra. He divided his time between Caer Idris and Talaith, spending many moonturns each Wintertide with the empress for the Light Celebrations and at the Crystal Palace during the summer. Unlike Zakael, Valterys showered the Crown Princess with attention. She blossomed into a lovely, kind-hearted child under his adopted fatherhood. The two even looked alike, with shocking black hair and pale skin. Only their eyes set them apart—his grey like a winter's sky, and hers a soft lavender. Everyone who met the princess commented on her unusual eyes. She would flutter her lashes and blush prettily at the compliments. Faelara was happy for Marissa. The girl had suffered loneliness and isolation in the palace with a mother more concerned with her crown than her daughter.

There were many courtiers who had befriended the princess, Fae and Rhoane among them, but a little girl should have peers her own age to play with. At least with Valterys, Marissa was able to have a father figure in her life. Faelara knew she was lucky to have a doting father in Brandt, and although she missed her mother greatly, wouldn't give up being raised by the man for anything.

When finally the empress announced she was with child, both kingdoms rejoiced. A few moonturns into Lliandra's pregnancy, Valterys left for Caer Idris with the promise he would return to the Crystal Palace before the birth. His absence distressed the princess, but the empress relaxed without the overlord's presence. Faelara sensed a disquiet in their relationship, which made this birth all the more precious.

The only person to hover over Lliandra more than Faelara was Myrddin. The two were constant companions of the empress. Faelara made certain there wasn't a miscarriage and did her best to keep both mother and child calm. Myrddin provided another kind of support to the empress. Less advisor, more like surrogate father, he coddled Lliandra with open displays of affection and concern. Never before had he troubled himself with Lliandra's childbearing, to which Faelara wondered if he, too, knew Valterys would father the Eirielle.

As the days passed and she witnessed Myrddin's concern for the empress turn from anxiousness to expectation, she reminded herself she really needed to have a chat with both Rhoane and Myrddin. Those two rogues were too good at keeping secrets and she hated being kept in the dark.

It wasn't just Myrddin whose excitement mounted as weeks turned to moonturns and the unborn baby continued to thrive. Even those who didn't know about the prophecy knew this child was special. Born of both Light and Dark. Never in the history of Aelinae had a child been born to two rulers of opposing kingdoms.

It was a new beginning.

CHAPTER SIXTEEN

Screams rent the summer air. Empress Lliandra thrashed upon the birthing bed, her face a torrent of pain. Rhoane fidgeted behind the modesty screen, where he and the others waited. Some waited for the birth of a new princess, another heir to solidify Lliandra's throne. Others waited for the birth of a prince, a link to the Obsidian Throne that would cement peace between the two kingdoms.

Rhoane cared little for a prince or another heir for the empress. He waited for the one foretold by Verdaine. The one who is and who is not. The Darennsai of his people.

His life mate.

His downfall.

Another cry, louder than the others and filled with anguish beyond pain, tore through his thoughts. He chanced a glance around the partition and saw the nursemaid shake her head. Lliandra sobbed as she turned from the sickening blue corpse of her infant son. The lifeless thing was placed in a basket to the side, away from the empress. A thin blanket covered their hopes and dreams.

Rhoane stared at the unmoving blanket. His mind whirled in

a tempest. How could Verdaine have it wrong? Surely the gods knew the future? She wouldn't have made him swear an oath if she were unsure. He'd lost more than his people for the unborn child. He'd lost his mother, his kingdom, and his homeland, taking the shame of being sheanna for the sake of Aelinae's future.

A future that now looked bleaker than ever. Peace would never be restored. Balance never regained. A malignant force wormed its way beneath the terrarae. He'd seen traces of the darkness too many times to discount the threat. He'd been certain this child, born of Valterys and Lliandra, the Lord of the Dark and the Lady of Light, would be his Darennsai.

The past twenty-five seasons had been spent preparing for her arrival. He'd done what Faisal asked and become more than a spy, more than an assassin. He'd murdered men and gathered information. He'd traveled to every corner of Aelinae, searching, studying, believing. And now those beliefs were in tatters. Lliandra had miscarried before—perhaps she and Valterys could have another child. But in his gut, Rhoane knew it was *this* pregnancy. *This* child. There wouldn't be a second chance.

Sickness roiled in his stomach. His hands shook with unfettered irritation. For a brief moment, he had the wild idea that he could give life to the stillborn child. To salvage what was lost.

"Your Majesty, there is another!"

The birthing woman's shout startled Rhoane. Another child. A twin. His gaze slid over the basket once more. Remorse for the dead infant tucked itself inside his heart.

Lliandra sobbed harder, her face a purplish mess of concentration and agony. The nurse pushed and prodded until a tiny pink body slithered into her hands. She held the newborn aloft and declared, "A princess!"

Relief, raw and scorching, swept over Rhoane. Something foreign bloomed in his chest and pinched his heart, unlocking what he'd painstakingly hidden away. *Hope.*

Nadra stepped from where she'd been hovering just beside the bed. A sword appeared in her hand and a collective gasp silenced the room. The goddess held Ynyd Eirathnacht, the sword Daknys had wielded in the Great War. The same sword that helped seal away her lover and betrayer, Rykoto. A sword embellished with two dragons.

Twice before Rhoane had witnessed the sword be presented. The dragons flanking the hilt glinted in the dim light and Rhoane thought he saw their wings flutter as Nadra held it aloft. Claidholm Solais hummed in his mind, singing a song he'd heard before, but had yet to decipher.

This was the one. This was the Darennsai. Tears stung the backs of his eyes and he willed them to dry. This was the reason he'd been born. For this child and for Aelinae. His desire to snatch the baby and run was almost too much to bear. He willed himself to stand still, his heart ramping up with each passing moment.

"No," Lliandra whispered, "not my daughter. Please. Not again. I cannot bear it."

"You know the prophecy as well as I. It must be done, if we are to be certain."

The nursemaid held the princess against her bosom, unsure what to do.

Ynyd Eirathnacht glowed white with ancient power. Claidholm Solais answered in kind, emanating power within the ornate scabbard Rhoane wore low on his hips. Rhoane absently hushed his weapon, keeping a trained eye on the other blade.

"Bring the child to me," Nadra commanded, and the nursemaid trembled as she pushed the tiny babe toward the goddess.

Lliandra lurched forward to snatch the princess. "Let me hold her once before you ruin all our lives." She breathed in the newborn, like a grierbas marking the scent of her young.

"Brandt," Nadra called, and the high priest stepped around

the gathered nobles to take the infant. "Place her right palm against the blade."

Brandt did as told, gingerly holding the tiny pink hand out toward the sword. When the infant's palm touched the metal, a light brighter than the sun blazed forth and the sword erupted in song. Those in the room covered their ears, but not Rhoane. He stood motionless and listened.

Although cut off from the ancients, he thought he heard their murmuring in his mind. The sword sang of a day when peace would blanket Aelinae and at last the land would be united as it was meant to be from the start. A peculiar rustling tickled his thoughts, like leathery wings unfurling in the wind. A voice, older than the terrarae and full of sorrow, whispered in his mind.

We will be here, our prince—waiting, watching. You are our last hope.

Rhoane stilled, willing the others to quiet so he might hear more, but the voice was gone, leaving a bitter taste in his mouth. *Remorse.* He knew that taste well. Had honed it like an aged wine until it became palatable. *Hope.* The voice had said he was their last hope. But who was he, and who were they? What did they wait for?

He patted his pocket, where the cynfar Verdaine had crafted for the Darennsai rested. All their hopes were as young and fragile as the infant princess, who stared in wide-eyed fascination at the sword.

"Please." Lliandra sobbed quietly. "Let her stay here. I promise I will raise her to be fair and without bias."

"You know I cannot do that." Nadra's musical voice undercut the words of the sword's song. "This child is the Eirielle and must be raised away from your or the other rulers' influence. It is the only way. We discussed this, my daughter."

"That was when I thought the child would be a boy and you would take him far from Valterys."

"Even so. We must protect Aelinae's future. It is the only way."

"Will I at least be able to visit her?" The empress's face contorted into a mask of rage and incredulity.

Nadra motioned to the nursemaid, who swaddled the princess in a fine woolen blanket. "No, my darling. You must never try to find her, lest your enemies learn of her existence. Everyone in this room will be compelled to forget the princess was born. When Valterys arrives tomorrow morning, he will find only his son. It is the only way I can protect her. Protect Aelinae."

"At least let me see my niece before you send her away." Duchess Gwyneira, so similar in coloring to her older sister but vastly different in temperament, took the infant from the nursemaid and bent low to whisper in her ear, "Fear not, little one. We are with you always. Though you may not see us, or hear us, we are in your heart. Remember this: there can be no Light without Dark, and no darkness without light. When you return to us, you will be our sun and moon, our stars and shadows. You will be Aelinae."

"What are you telling her? Give me my daughter." Lliandra held her hands out to take the baby, and Gwyneira obliged, but not before she placed her lips upon the little princess's.

As she bent to give the child to her sister, she grimaced and put a hand on her swollen belly. "Gods be willing, there might be need of the nursemaids once more tonight."

Nadra placed a protective hand over Gwyneira's. "Nay, my love, your child will be born in two days hence. He is excited to be near his cousin."

"He?" Gwyneira cast a sly glance at her husband, Duke Anje. "And you swore it was a daughter."

Anje winked at his wife. "I said I welcomed a child, male or female. Either would be equally loved."

"Yes, and you also said you wanted a daughter to spoil."

"It is time," Nadra interrupted, indicating to Brandt that he should take the baby.

"But why Father?" Faelara asked. "Why not Myrddin? He's older than all of us and almost as powerful as the empress. Surely he would be the best caregiver for the child."

"Myrddin and I have discussed this," Nadra began, "and it's been decided Brandt is better suited to raising a child on his own. Myrddin, as you know, has no offspring, and although his powers are great, his paternal skills are not." The last was said with a smile warm enough to brighten the leaden skies.

"It is only for a few seasons," Myrddin added. "You will see your father again before you know it."

A tear streaked down Faelara's cheek, and she sniffed. "Yes, I know. I'm being quite selfish, and I apologize. Don't do anything foolish, Father. Bring the princess home safely." She stood on tiptoe to kiss the high priest. "I love you."

"And I you, my dearest." Brandt hugged the child to his chest and wrapped his other arm around his only daughter. "I will think of you every day."

"Rhoane," Nadra said, "you will accompany Brandt."

"It will be my honor." Rhoane bowed low to Lliandra, then to the others in the room. Voices rose in a chatter of dismay. Lliandra's sobs were stifled beneath requests for one last cuddle, one final kiss, but Nadra ignored all of them.

As Rhoane left the birthing chamber with Brandt, he heard Nadra whisper, "You shall forget this child. Erase her from your mind so she can be safe."

They sped away from the palace, Brandt on a sturdy gelding and Rhoane on his stallion. They had no clothing and no food for the infant, and no idea where Nadra wished them to go. They rode through the night, headed west toward the Spine of Ohlin. Every so often Rhoane would check behind them, but they were not followed. Not that he'd expected anyone to ride after them, but he'd learned long ago to be cautious just the same.

We're to meet Nadra in the cavern. Brandt's gravelly thought brushed against Rhoane's mind.

Then I shall get us there without delay.

He folded time and before the sun rose in the west, they were several days from Talaith. The baby slept most of the night, tucked safely in the warm confines of Brandt's tunic, but with the dawn came her hunger.

"We must find some milk for the babe," Brandt said as they approached a farmhouse on the outskirts of a small village.

Rhoane scanned the barn and listened for sounds of livestock. At the bleat of a goat, he prodded Lucitan. "There is fresh milk to be had in there." He pointed toward the well-made building. "The farmer is not yet awake. We have a small amount of time to procure what we need."

They hurried to the barn and tethered their horses to a stall inside. Brandt kept watch while Rhoane filled two wineskins with warm milk. He fashioned a nipple by wrapping cheesecloth around the tip. Brandt held the bottle to the princess, and she drank hungrily for several minutes before she settled into a satisfied sleep.

"We must make haste. The farmer will wake soon." Rhoane cocked his head as he listened for any sound to cause alarm. Hearing none, they reclaimed their mounts and raced from the farmstead toward Mount Nadrene.

Rhoane folded time once more, and they sped through towns and villages, unseen by others. To them, he and Brandt were but a trip of the light, something glimpsed and then forgotten. If they even noticed at all. Still, Rhoane couldn't shake the feeling something tracked them on their race to the cavern. Not Aelan, nor Fadair, nor even man or beast. Something malevolent that whispered through the trees. Rhoane eased his stallion closer to Brandt and placed a protective ward of his ShantiMari around them.

Brandt's stern face was set in a grimace as he clutched the

child to his chest. "Do you sense it as well?" he asked through clenched teeth.

"Aye. Whatever it is, it is immune to my power. We should be at the cavern by nightfall. Have you the strength to carry on?"

"Don't worry about me, lad. I'm not as old as I look." They both chuckled at that. Brandt was older than Rhoane by at least a century, but had the health and stamina of a man of mid-age.

Dark clouds funneled over the fields, and Rhoane cursed the summer rainstorms prevalent this season. Mid-summer was a time for sunshine and Light. Not the dire rain and darkness haunting their days of late. He glanced at the sleeping babe in Brandt's arms. Gods, but he hoped the prophecy was true. He hoped this child was the bringer of balance to Aelinae, and not the destruction of them all.

They reached the hidden cavern entrance and let their horses loose in a small grove of trees. Together, they painstakingly made their way to the sacred space nestled deep in the mountain. Nadra waited for them on the bank of the great lake that sprawled to the cavern's depths. Rhoane had visited the cavern several times in the long seasons he waited for the Darennsai's birth. Each time he saw the clear waters of the lake, his tension and anxiety unfurled from him like a darathi vorsi stretching its wings.

He wordlessly took the child from Brandt's embrace and removed the woolen blanket. She wriggled in his grip, squirming to recover the warmth. He shushed her and held her against his tunic until she quieted, then gently dipped her into the lake. Her deep-blue eyes grew large against her tiny face. He sang in Eleri, a song of devotion.

When she was fully submerged, he smoothed his hand over her nakedness, washing away the taint of Aelinae. She needed to begin her new life innocent of every expectation, hope, and demand he saw in her future.

He lifted her from the water and chuckled at her wild-eyed

sputtering. "I would never hurt you, *Darennsai*." His ShantiMari curled around her, warming her skin, providing comfort and protection that would last far into the future. "*Nyath minas, ninyeh Taen das laerl. Dinyath allundrel kneesh awl hap teergartn.* My heart, my sword, my life is yours, sweet *Darennsai*." He reached into his pocket and removed the cynfar Verdaine had given him. In all the seasons since he'd left the Narthvier, he'd carried it. As he placed it around her neck, he heard the dulcet tones of another song, not from his sword, but the pendant. His words had bound him to her. The song wrapped around him, into him, through him.

She peered up at him as if understanding what was happening. Intelligence shone in her eyes, and he recalled his vision on the beach. "Be brave, little one. I will be here when you return. I promise." His lips brushed the smooth skin of her forehead, and he inhaled her scent deeply, imprinting it on his heart.

"Please, can I know her name?"

Nadra brushed the soft curls on the infant's head. "She is called Taryn Rose."

"Taryn," Rhoane whispered, "I will wait for you. Remember me."

He handed the child to Brandt and knew in the depths of his being he would honor his oath to Verdaine. If he had to wait ten thousand lifetimes for her—for Taryn—he would. Together they would bring balance to Aelinae.

He finally understood what that meant. Without him she would fail, but that wasn't the whole of the prophecy. He needed her as well. To accomplish his task, he required her strength. Not just her strength, but her unconditional love. Without her, he would fail.

You will betray her not once, but twice.

He ignored the taunt and replaced it with his own version of the future. They would heal Aelinae together. In him was the remedy. After all, he was the Prince of Dragons.

CHAPTER SEVENTEEN

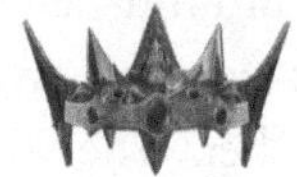

Crown Princess Marissa crept through the silent halls of her mother's massive palace. At this time of night, the nobles were either sleeping or carousing in one another's beds. A few servants scampered down darkened hallways, but no one saw her. At least, she hoped they didn't.

She'd woken from a dream of her mother screaming, yet when she checked her mother's sleeping quarters, the bed was empty. This close to the baby's arrival date, Marissa knew it could only mean one thing—the child had come early. Valterys's son. Her stepfather would be arriving in the morning, and Marissa imagined the pleased smile on his face when he held the baby. He was a caring, loving father who had shown her nothing but kindness.

Over the course of a decade, he'd become the father she'd wished for, the loving parent she'd craved. He showered her with attention and affection, the two things her mother either couldn't or wouldn't give.

A creak on the stairs alerted her a moment before the courtier rushed past. She pressed herself against the wall, too terrified to breathe. If her mother caught her sneaking into the birthing chamber, she'd be punished with more than just words. Lliandra had made it clear Marissa was to be nowhere near the chamber when the little prince was born. Something about having all the heirs too close together and safety, but it was nonsense.

Marissa knew her mother. Knew Lliandra didn't want Marissa to bond with her little brother before Valterys took him away. A vague memory of a chubby cheeked little boy with chestnut hair and an impish smile pricked her nerves. He'd been in her dreams often of late, but she had no idea who he was. It didn't matter. She had a brother to think about now.

Little did the empress know, Valterys had already promised Marissa her own suite of rooms at Caer Idris and the offer to visit any time she liked. He'd even shown her how to transform into a great feiche, so she could fly there in the space of a night. Lliandra was a fool to think she could keep Marissa from her brother. Just like she was a fool to think she could control Marissa's growing desires.

The empty hallway to the birthing chamber gave Marissa pause. There should be guards outside the doors. Servants, perhaps—definitely odas, the women trained in the art of bringing babies safely into the world. The constant pelt of rain against the windows was the only sound. No screams, no joyous chattering.

Marissa glanced up and down the long corridor before she placed a tentative hand on the door handle. A wave of nausea swept over her. She snatched her hand away. The door was warded against anyone entering. But why?

She felt along the metal of the doorknob, sensing the Shanti-Mari that bound the door closed. Untying power was much like untangling a necklace. It took time, patience, and nimble fingers. Even though she couldn't see the ShantiMari, her own power could work through the bindings. Usually. This power was unlike any she'd come across before.

Marissa stepped back and surveyed the door. It was much the

same as the others in the palace—painted white with gold trim. Nothing about the door indicated what the room beyond was used for. If a visitor to the palace didn't know their way around, they would walk past none the wiser. But tonight there was something extraordinary going on inside, and she was going to find out what.

The clack of sturdy work shoes sounded against the marble floor, and Marissa scurried to a darkened alcove. A serving girl approached the door and entered without any resistance. For the briefest moment, Marissa heard the frantic whispers from within. The baby was coming!

Once more she tried the door, only to be blocked by an unseen force. Undaunted, she prowled the adjoining corridor until she found a secret entrance that led to cramped and musty passageways. The entire palace had inner walkways. No longer in use, the first empress had had them built behind the walls to prevent nobles from being disturbed by servants. Over the seasons, the corridors were used more for the nobles' illicit encounters than for keeping servants out of sight. Marissa knew the passageways well. Especially the rooms where her mother's courtiers took their lovers when they didn't want to be discovered.

But that was on the far side of the palace, and not what Marissa was interested in at the moment. She flicked her wrist, and a flame of her Mari sparked to life to illuminate the tiny space. Beyond the wall to her left, she heard movement and followed the sound until she came to another secret doorway. On the other side of the wall, the door was concealed by a heavy tapestry. One she detested but her mother loved. It showed a scene from the Great War, of Rykoto being imprisoned into the Temple of Ardyn with the elder gods watching as Nadra set the final seal into a column. The anguish on Rykoto's face had caused Marissa to have night frights.

Not because she feared the mad god, but because she felt sorry for him.

She pressed the latch and held her breath as it creaked open. When no one came looking for the cause of the sound, she slid behind the tapestry and inched her way to the edge of the fabric.

A shriek that could split the hairs on a carlix's tail froze Marissa in place. Mother. The baby.

Marissa eased her head from behind the tapestry to glimpse the room. What she saw stole her breath. A cry rose to her lips, but she bit her tongue to keep silent.

There, in a basket carelessly set away from the birthing bed, was her brother. A thin blanket covered the tiny thing, but she could clearly make out the shape of his face, his tiny hands—his maleness, even. The thrall of death clung to his inert form.

Another cry from her mother caused her to glance toward the bed, where she saw the oda's arms disappear between the empress's legs to coax another child into the world.

Twins.

Keeping to the shadows and crouching low so as not to be seen, Marissa crept to the basket and lifted the blanket to gaze upon the still face of her dead brother. A blue tint marred his perfection. Marissa stifled a sob and covered the little thing.

"Please," Marissa heard her mother beg. "Let her stay here. I promise I will raise her to be fair and without bias."

A sister. No, gods please, not a sister.

"You know I cannot do that." Nadra's tone held a hint of anger, and Marissa gave the others her full attention.

What happened next played out like a fantastical drama on the stage. Slivers of terror wormed their way to her core as she watched the high priest place the infant's palm upon the blade of Nadra's great sword. A blinding light burst forth, and Marissa cowered in the corner, afraid of being discovered. Tears squeezed from between her closed eyes and dripped from her chin to the thick carpets.

The Eirielle was supposed to be a boy. Valterys's son. He would be taken to Caer Idris, and Marissa would help raise him. It was as she and Valterys had planned.

But the gods cared little for her, it seemed.

A screeching came from the sword, and she covered her ears against the horrid sound. When at last it ceased its wretched noise, she stayed still, watching as the others bent to give the princess kisses. Before the last cuddle was given, Marissa, on hands and knees, returned to the tapestry. She gave one last glance to her mother before she saw Brandt and Rhoane slip from the room.

She shut the door to Nadra's command that the others forget about the princess.

Marissa would never forget. Never forget her mother let the goddess steal her child to be raised…where? With the Eleri? Why else would Rhoane accompany the high priest? Or would they take the baby to the Sitari? Let her be raised as a savage warrior until she was…what? Needed to defeat Valterys? What was her mother planning?

Questions raced through her mind as quickly as her slippered feet sped her through the palace. Once returned to her rooms, she paced the sitting area, thinking, plotting. She went to the window and looked out over the seas toward the Summerlands. She would need them, but not yet. There was time to plan, to do this right. Lliandra might have custody of the Eirielle, but Marissa was the Crown Princess. She would control the court. Someday she would have her own heirs and rule Talaith as the rightful empress.

She placed a hand over her belly. At seventeen seasons, she was still a maiden, as was tradition. But with the next Wintertide, her mother would take her to a house where she would be introduced to the ways of lovemaking. An empress of Talaith had many lovers and must be skilled in the use of her body for not just creating heirs. Of course, she would not be able to conceive a child until well into her hundredth season or so, but surely there were ways to encourage her body to bear children sooner.

And why wait until her eighteenth Wintertide? Marissa turned toward the west and grinned. She would lose her maidenhead on her own terms, and she knew exactly who would be her first. Satisfied for the moment, she crawled beneath the sheets of her huge bed.

When her maids woke her the next morning, it was with the sad news that the empress had delivered a stillborn prince. Marissa wept pretty tears and said all the right words, but inside she buried her anguish.

She waited outside her mother's apartments as she listened to the tirade Valterys heaped upon the empress. He was furious to be met with a dead child, and Marissa was certain half the palace heard him.

The two guards stationed outside Lliandra's doors never flinched, but she saw in their eyes the desire to protect their empress. The Lord of the Dark was an imposing man, but her mother could handle him. She always had.

"Spying, Princess?"

Marissa turned at the seductive voice beckoning her. "Of course not, Prince Zakael. I'm waiting to pay my respects to Mother."

Zakael's lips tightened to a thin line. "Don't call me that."

"But you are a prince. It's ridiculous the ruler of the east is an empress, but the ruler of the west be called an overlord. That's a stupid tradition, if you ask me."

"No one asked you, did they?"

Marissa bit her tongue against the harsh retort that sprang to her lips. "Please, let's not quarrel." She cocked her head toward the empress's suite. "They're doing enough of that for both kingdoms."

Zakael's glance slid from the closed door to her face, and then, as she hoped, to her barely concealed breasts. "They should be allies, not enemies," he drawled, distracted. "Princess, it's been too long since we've seen each other. Perhaps we should reacquaint ourselves."

Marissa drew in a deep breath and lifted her chin. At thirty seasons, Zakael was not yet emancipated from his father, but she knew that mattered little to the man. He did as he pleased, often disappearing from court for weeks. Rumors abounded about his randy behavior, and some even said the Lord of the Dark had given his son a castle to use as he wished. Partly as a way to keep Zakael from his dealings at court, and partly as a means to avoid witnessing what his son did for pleasure.

A flush of heat started at Marissa's sternum and crept up to her face. If the rumors were true, and Zakael was as vile as they said, she wanted to consume his poison.

She led Zakael away from her mother's apartments and the ever-present ears of her guards to a lesser-used part of the palace, where she knew they would not be disturbed. After she checked the locks on every door of the spacious sitting room, Marissa returned to where she'd left Zakael standing beside an ornate couch.

"I have a favor to ask." She looked up at him from beneath a thick fringe of lashes and placed her fingertips at the ties of her bodice. She fought to control the trembling of her knees and stutter of her voice. If he denied her, all would be lost. Too much rested on Zakael's response to her request.

"As a rule, I don't like favors. They imply a quid pro quo, and I'm not one for being indebted to anyone. But if you're the one asking, you'd be indebted to me, and I rather like that."

She unlaced her gown and shrugged out of it until it fell to the floor. Heat lit the depths of Zakael's eyes, encouraging her to continue. "As you know, I'm six moonturns from turning eighteen Wintertides. At such time, my mother will take me to a house where I'll be fully versed in the ways of making love." She slipped her chemise over her heavy breasts and across her hips until it, too, lay in a pile at her feet. Her pale body shivered against the sudden chill on her naked skin. "I don't wish to wait that long to lose my maidenhood."

"Princess, this is ludicrous. If your mother finds out, she'll have me beheaded." His gruff words did not match the lust in his eyes.

"Are you saying you don't wish to take my virginity?" She ran a hand over her breast and pinched her nipple. The bulge in his pants answered for him. "I thought as much. Make love to me, Zakael. Wrap me in your Dark power until I can't breathe. Satisfy me like only you can, and I will tell you a secret."

He raised his slate-colored eyes, filled now with fire and passion, to stare into her lavender orbs. "What secret?"

"Afterward, I'll tell you. First, you must make me scream with passion and lust and all the things I've been told happens between a man and woman. You must make me believe I am desired beyond all others. Do you understand?"

His mouth crushed hers, and she tasted blood. His tongue ravaged against her lips, and she opened herself to his brutal exploration. A rough hand massaged her breast before he pinched her nipple harder than she ever had. A cry buried itself in the confines of his mouth, and his lips quirked in a smile as they kissed. The rumors were true—Zakael liked pain.

A throbbing down low webbed its way outward to her extremities until she grasped at his trousers and yanked the ties loose. Yes, he was the perfect choice. He was cruel and brutal and everything she admired. All those seasons of following him around had taught her that Zakael was her equal. Without knowing it, he had taught her how to subtly manipulate someone to do her bidding. She'd perfected the art and now, he'd teach her how to use her body. And later, after he satisfied her beyond reason, she would tell him of the other child—the secret princess her mother had hidden.

Once Valterys's rage ran its course, she and Zakael would tell him of the princess, and together, the three of them would find the child.

Their plans were merely delayed, not destroyed.

EPILOGUE

The veil was as the veil had always been—a haze of mist between the worlds. Except, much had happened in the course of a few short seasons. Gilchrist raised his snout and sniffed the air. A grin stretched the scales of his lips.

Yes, much had happened since he saw the birth of the prince. Although the lad didn't know what it meant to be their savior, he would soon enough. There was still time.

Ahmbra fluttered to the ground. Her flying skills improved with each day. Upon her back rode the queen. He shuddered to recall how he'd watched in horror as she sacrificed herself. Blue flames had engulfed her body and her screams had made his ears bleed.

But then the goddess Verdaine had held her like a mother her sleeping child and brought her to them. She'd laid the stricken queen upon the ground at Jinnipher's talons.

"Heal her," the goddess had commanded. "Your future and that of your prince requires it."

That first night, Gilchrist and Ahmbra had taken turns watching over the Eleri, while Jinnipher healed the woman with her tears. Each teardrop blossomed on the queen's pale skin, like a night-blooming rose in summer. Every consecutive blossom blended with the next until the savage burns were no more.

When she woke, a fortnight or so later, her eyes were haunted, her expression one of great sadness.

Gilchrist had done his best to comfort her, as had all the darathi vorsi, but she mourned the loss of her family and her homeland. It took many seasons before gaiety entered her smiles. He held each one of them in his heart, cherished like a gift.

And now he hoped his news would lighten her sorrows even more.

The young darathi giggled as only the innocent could and fluttered her wings. "We found more grazing pastures beyond the fifth canyon." Ahmbra's eyes glittered with excitement. She and the queen had been scouting for new places where they might have a better chance of survival. But Gilchrist was reluctant to leave this place, where he caught glimpses into his home world.

"Come now, old dragon, what has you vexed this morning?" The queen stroked his long neck and his scales rippled at her touch.

"Look." He indicated the veil that separated them from Aelinae. "The Darennsai. She's come."

Aislinn gasped and put a hand to her chest. "Rhoane." The whispered name traveled on the breeze across the canyon. "Can you see him?"

"Aye. He is well." Gilchrist watched Nadra place the child in an old man's arms and send them through a glimmering doorway. That was the last he saw of the princess, but he knew, wherever the Great Mother had sent her, she was safe.

Tears streamed down Aislinn's cheeks to drip from her chin and plop upon the dusty ground. And there, at her feet, tiny green tendrils sprang from the terrarae. They sprouted to slim stalks, getting thicker with each breath she took until a bed of white roses bloomed before her.

Ahmbra gasped and looked to him for an answer. For the first time in his long life, he had no explanation of what was happening.

Aislinn clapped her hands and danced around the flowers. Her long hair flew behind her like a dragon's wing. Jinnipher joined them, as did several of their brethren, snorting fire from their snouts and flapping their wings in long-awaited jubilation. The Darennsai had come at last and soon, when the Prince of Dragons wore the Crown of Awakening, they could return to Aelinae.

CAST OF CHARACTERS

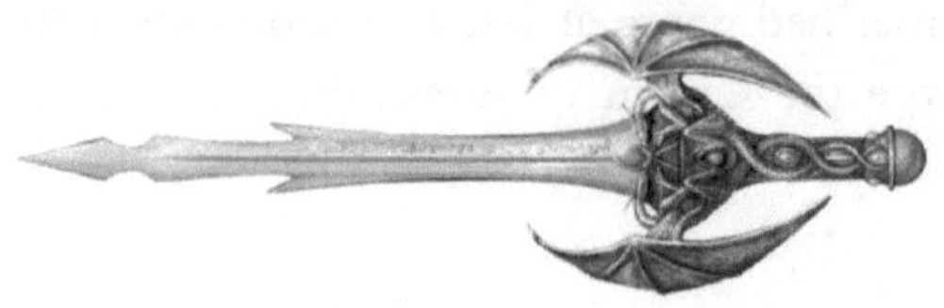

Ahmbra (Amm-brah) ~ A golden darathi vorsi living in exile. Conceived on Aelinae, she was born in exile and is the last of her kind.

Aislinn al Glennwoods ap Narthvier (Ay-s-lynn) ~ Queen of the Eleri. Married to Stephen ap Narthvier. Aislinn perished in a ShantiMari accident when Rhoane was a young man.

Alswyth Myrddin (Alls-with Mere-din) ~ Mage with exceedingly long life. Myrddin is the advisor to Empress Lliandra and is often far from court on assignments from the crown. No known children or spouses. No known House.

Amdi Agnar ~ Laird of the Ullan tribes. He claimed Kaleigh as his consort and has two sons with her. Descendent of House Agnar.

Anje ap Paderau (Ann-jee ap Paw-der-oo) ~ Becomes Duke of Paderau upon his marriage to Gwyneira. Anje is cousin to the Lord of the Dark, and third in line for the Obsidian Throne. His father was brother to Valterys's father. A prince in his own right, Anje renounced his Dark heritage to live with his wife in the Light. Descendant of House Djeba.

Baldev de Deistra (Ball-dev de Des-tra) ~ King of the

Seas. Baldev lives within a vast complex at the bottom of the ocean. Merfolk are believed to be legends as they are not often seen. Once a year, on their naming day, merfolk have the option to walk among the other races on Aelinae. It is unknown if Baldev has ever honored the tradition. Married to Salaria. Father to several daughters and sons. Descendent of House Deistra.

Baehlon de Monteferron (Bay-lohn de Mont-fair-on) ~ Danuri and Geigan knight employed by Empress Lliandra. Descendant of House Monteferron.

Brandt Kaj Endion (Brant) ~ Aelan. High Priest of Talaith and advisor to Empress Lliandra, Brandt was commissioned with Taryn's safety when she was born. House Arran.

Bressal ap Narthvier (Bress-all) ~ Eleri. Second Son to King Stephan and Queen Aislinn.

Carga ap Narthvier ~ Eleri. Initiate to Verdaine's High Priestess. Daughter to King Stephan and Queen Aislinn.

Daknys (Dak-niss) ~ Elder Goddess. Daughter of Nadra and Ohlin, she is worshipped by the Light and Dark in the central area of Aelinae.

Deshan Agnar (Day-shawn Ag-nar) ~ Ullan. Deceased laird of the Ullans. Brother to Amdi Agnar.

Eoghan ap Narthvier (Eee-gan) ~ Eleri. Third Son to King Stephan and Queen Aislinn.

Esna fei Garrith (Ez-nah fay Gare-eth) ~ Danurian. Minor noble who attracted Lliandra's attention. Fathered a son with the empress (Kane, not named in books) and Marissa, the crown princess. Was executed for trying to poison the empress. Descendent of House Garrith.

Faelara Dal Arran (Fay-lara) ~ Aelan. Daughter of Brandt, Faelara is currently a lady-in-waiting to Empress Lliandra. Her Healing skills are legendary, as are her father's. House Arran.

Faisal dei Tarnovo (Fay-sal) ~ Summerlander. King of the Summerlands. House Tarnov.

Gilchrist (Gill-krisst) ~ Elder darathi vorsi living in exile. Mate to Jinnipher.

Gwyneira Tjaru ap Paderau (Gwin-eera ap Shar-U) ~ Aelan. Sister to Empress Lliandra, wife of Duke Anje. Houses Nadrene and Djeba.

Hanan ~ A Summerlands merchant living in Menurra.

Ivyn (Eye-vin) ~ A pirate captain of undetermined heritage.

Janeira (Juh-nair-a) ~ An Eleri warrior of great standing, excellent skill, and deadly capabilities.

Jayden dei Tarnovo ~ Fist born son to King Faisal and Queen Prateeni of the Summerlands. Heir to the Summerlands throne. House Tarnov.

Jinnipher (Gin-i-fur) ~ A darathi vorsi living in exile. Mate to Gilchrist.

Julieta ~ Younger Goddess. Daughter of Rykoto and Daknys.

Kaleigh al Fyrnwood ap Agnar (Kay-lee) ~ Eleri. Sheanna living among the Ullans. The sworn concubine to Laird Amdi. Kaleigh has two sons with the laird.

Kragor (Kray-gore) ~ Geigan. A brutish man Rhoane fights in the arena.

Lliandra Tjaru (Lee-on-dra Shar-U) ~ Aelan. Empress of Talaith, Lady of Light. Mother to Marissa, Taryn, Eliahnna, and Tessa. Lliandra is directly descended from the goddess Nadra. She is thought to be a just ruler who thinks of her subjects in all matters. House Nadrene.

Lucitan (Loose-eh-tahn) ~ Rhoane's Ullan stallion, given to him by Amdi Agnar.

Mallaqai (Mahl-ah-k-eye) ~ Believed to be a witch, Mallaqai betrayed the *darathi vorsi* during the Great War and caused their disappearance from Aelinae. Death is unknown, whereabouts is unknown. Believed to have perished in the Great War, Mallaqai has not been seen or heard from since.

Marissa Tjaru (Shar-U) ~ Aelan. Crown Princess of Talaith, heir to the Light Throne, daughter of Lliandra and Esna. Descendant of House Nadrene.

Micha Askell (Mike-uh Ask-elle) ~ Aelan. Baehlon's intended wife. Daughter of Lord Askell. House Askell.

Nadra ~ Goddess. Mother of Aelinae, Great Mother of all Creation. Along with Ohlin, Nadra created Aelinae. Mother to Daknys, Rykoto, Kaldaar, and Verdaine.

Ohlin (O-lynn) ~ God. Father of Aelinae, Great Father of all Creation. Along with Nadra, Ohlin created Aelinae. Father to to Daknys, Rykoto, Kaldaar, and Verdaine.

Prateeni dei Tarnovo (Pruh-teen-ee) ~ Summerlander. Queen of the Summerlands. House Tarnov.

Rhoane al Glennwoods ap Narthvier (Rone) ~ Eleri. First Son of Stephan, King of the Eleri, and Aislinn, Queen of the Eleri. At birth Rhoane was prophesied to be the Eirielle's protector. When he was a young lad, he took an oath forsaking all others and devoting his life to upholding Verdaine's prophecy.

Rykoto (Ree-ko-toe) ~ Elder God. Son of Nadra and Ohlin, worshipped by inhabitants of the Northwest and of the Dark. Rykoto was imprisoned in the Temple of Ardyn after the Great War.

Stephan ap Narthvier (Steff-ahn) ~ King of the Eleri. Married to Aislinn. Father to Rhoane, Bressal, Carga, and Eoghan. Stephan firmly believes the Eleri are stronger on their own, away from the other races of Aelinae. He opposes the Verdaine's prophecy regarding his son, Rhoane.

Troyanna Djeba ~ Wife to Valterys Djeba, mother to Zakael. House Djeba.

Valterys Djeba (Val-terr-iss D-jj-ay-ba) ~ Aelan. Overlord of the West, Lord of the Dark. Father to Taryn and Zakael. Valterys is directly descended from the god Ohlin. He rules his kingdom with a tight grasp on its economy and trade. His subjects think of him favorably. House Djeba.

Verdaine (Vare-dane) ~ Elder Goddess. Daughter of Nadra and Ohlin, she is worshipped by the Eleri in the Narthvier.

Zakael Djeba (Zah-K-ay-el D-jj-ay-ba) ~ Aelan. Prince, heir to the Obsidian Throne. Son of Valterys and Troyanna (not named in books). Descendant of House Djeba.

GLOSSARY OF TERMS

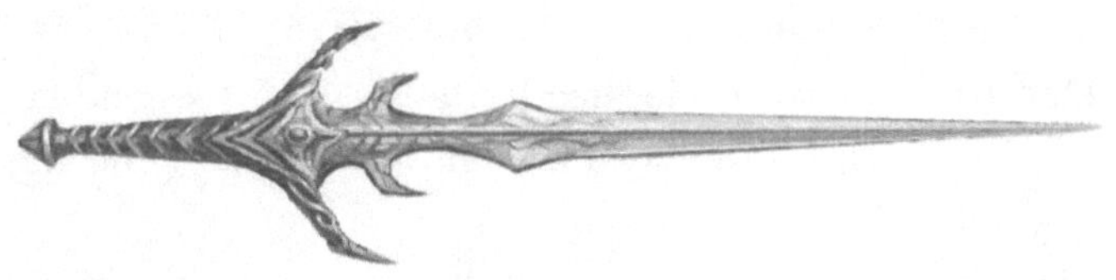

Aelinae (Ay-lynn-ay) ~ A world created by Nadra and Ohlin. It is disk-shaped with waterfalls at the edge of the world, and volcanoes beneath it.

Artagh (R-tah-g) ~ Related to the Eleri, Artaghs lack the Eleri Glamour, as well as the sophistication of the ancient race. They are rumored to be the best at making weapons and working with metals, especially the fabled Godsteel found only in the Haversham Mountains. Outsiders are often distrusted and it's rare to find Artaghs far from their caves.

Bells Aelinae's form of time telling. One bell is one Aelinean hour.

Caer Idris (Care Ee-dris) ~ The ancestral home of The Overlord of the West. Currently, Valterys, Lord of the Dark sits on the Obsidian Throne.

Claidholm Solais (Kleeve Solish) ~ Sword of Light. Ohlin had this sword made for his daughter Verdaine during the Great War, but she refused to use it.

Carlix ~ A sleek, winged feline who makes her home in the mountains known as the Spine of Ohlin. One of the first creatures to inhabit the planet of Aelinae. Often referred to for their flexibility and quick responses, the number of people who have actually seen a carlix is few.

Dal Ferran (Dahl Fair-en) ~ The fiery pits of hell beneath Aelinae's surface.

Dal Tara (Dahl Tar-a) ~ A celestial resting place for the Gods and those they deem worthy. It is located in the second quadrant of the Meirdia Nebula.

Danuri ~ A Province located in the West. The second largest city to Caer Idris, Danuri is widely known for their wine and ale making skills.

Darathi Vorsi (Dah-rahth-ee Vor-see) ~ Aside from the carlix, *darathi vorsi* are the oldest creatures on Aelinae. Several thousand seasons ago they disappeared from the planet, but the Eleri hold the belief that one day they will return.

Darathi Eneari (Dah-rahth-ee Enn-ee-rie) ~ The *darathi eneari* have been lost to legend. As old as the darathi vorsi, these water dragons have not been seen in thousands of seasons, thus earning them mythical status.

Darennsai (Dar-en-sigh) ~ An ancient title given to Taryn by the Eleri. Most don't know the true meaning of the word, thinking of it as nothing more than an honorific bestowed upon her by the Goddess Verdaine. Only a few know the word means, Daughter of the Sky. Less an oath than a promise that one day Taryn will sit at the side of Verdaine, as a goddess in her own right. The Eleri reject this idea.

Eirielle (Air-ee-elle) ~ The one of prophecy. Said to be the destroyer or the savior of Aelinae, depending on which prophecy you read. Only one Eirielle is ever said to be created, but that doesn't stop those of the Light and Dark from trying to make others. The Eirielle is rumored to possess all the strands of Shanti-Mari: Light, Dark, Eleri, and Telraicht-Noir. Although, the last is only known to the Brotherhood.

Eleri (Ee-ler-ee) ~ A mysterious clan of elf-like men and women who live in the Narthvier. They stay within the borders of their forest and don't like outsiders coming on their land. The Eleri share a collective conscious, in that they can call on the wisdom of past and future Eleri in times of duress. The oldest race on Aelinae, they and the *darathi vorsi* share a common bond. Thought to be caretakers of the beasts, when the *darathi vorsi* disappeared, it was a time of great mourning for the Eleri.

Fadair (Fah-d-air) ~ The name Eleri have given to anyone not Eleri. It is meant to be used as a way to signify someone not of Eleri descent, but often it is used as a disparaging slur against non-Eleri.

Genari (Gen-ar-ee) ~ The Summerlands term for midwife.

Glamour ~ A slight shimmering beneath the skin. Found only on Eleri.

Grhom (Gr-om) ~ A spiced drink made by the Eleri. It has healing properties and gives strength through the many ingredients used to make it. Occasionally, the Eleri will add alcohol to the drink.

Grierbas (Greer-bah) ~ A large, wolf-like animal that makes its home in the Narthvier. Wild and territorial, grierbas keep away from civilizations, even avoiding the Eleri.

Lan Gyllarelle (Lahn Gill-a-rell) ~ A vast lake located in the Narthvier. Its waters are rumored to hold healing properties. The Eleri often hold ceremonies on the banks of the lake.

Levon (Le-von) ~ A sleek black bird. Faster than any other birds, the levon is a favorite form of transportation for those competent in transformation.

Menurra ~ The capital city of the Summerlands. Located on the main island, it is the ancestral home to the king and queen of the Summerlands.

Narthvier (Narth-veer) ~ A vast forest covering the northeast portion of Aelinae. The Eleri make their home in the Narthvier, or vier as some call it. The Eleri are protective of the forest and use veils to dissuade unwelcome visitors. Only the Eleri know how to raise the fabled veils.

Oda ~ Talaithian midwife.

Plenta ~ An Eleri pastry filled with sausage and cheese.

Sheanna (Shee-ahn-a) ~ An exiled Eleri. When an Eleri is *sheanna*, they are required to cut their hair and live outside the borders of the Narthvier until a certain amount of time has passed. Once they return to the Narthvier, they must complete the purification ceremony before they are considered to be Eleri once more.

ShantiMari (Shahn-tee Mar-ee) ~ Two halves of the same whole. ShantiMari is a power found in all things on Aelinae. Within men and women, it manifests itself in varying degrees from no visible signs, to extremely powerful. Those in positions of great power will have more ShantiMari than those born to the lesser clans or Houses. The Trinity of Power is made up of Light (female), Dark (male), and Eleri (either male or female, Eleri ShantiMari is culled from nature). Within the confines of Shanti-Mari are rules, or etiquette. The power can be culled from the smallest pebble to the stars themselves. Wielding more power than one is capable of controlling often leads to a painful death.

Sitari (Sit-ar-ee) ~ Blue skinned warrior women who live in a community devoid of men. Their island sits at the southernmost edge of Aelinae. It is rumored their preferred mates are Geigan males. Sitari women can be found in other kingdoms of Aelinae, usually scouting for the strongest to procreate with. Once coupling has been achieved, the Sitari return to their island. Male offspring are said to be sacrificed to their goddess.

Summerlands ~ An island kingdom located south of Talaith in the Summer Seas.

Summer Seas ~ The body of water covering the entire southern area of Aelinae.

Surtentse (Sir-tants) ~ An ancient title meaning 'Son of the Terrarae'. Verdaine gives this honorific to Rhoane.

Talaith (Tal - eth) ~ The capital city of the East. Ruled by the empress, also known as The Lady of Light.

Terrarae ~ Aelinean name for earth, or ground. The substance upon which life is built.

The East ~ A geographical location on the map indicating all lands, properties, kingdoms, etc east of the Spine of Ohlin. Includes the Narthvier, Ulla, Talaith, and the marshes near Kaldaar's Stones.

Ulla (Oo-la) ~ A kingdom located in the far East of Aelinae. The Ullans are a tribal people, following their herds throughout the season. Ullan horses are of the finest stock.

Verdaine's Prophecy ~ When Rhoane was born, Verdaine prophesied that he would be exiled from his people until the *gyota* returned. His fate would be tied to the one who is and who is not for all time.

Vorlock ~ A huge, lizard-like creature with heavy scales and a wide frill around its head. Vorlocks contain a poison that can kill a man or woman instantly.

Weirren (Weer-en) ~ The ancestral home of the Eleri King and Queen.

Weirren Court ~ The gathered nobility of the Eleri live among the many buildings interwoven through the ancient tree that makes up the Weirren.

Weirren Throne ~ Built into the oldest tree on Aelinae, the Weirren Throne is a living, breathing seat.

Ynyd Eirathnacht (Inid Air-ath-nack-t) ~ Sword of Dark. Ohlin had this sword made for his daughter Daknys during the Great War. She used it to help seal Rykoto in his prison. Its current location is unknown.

AUTHOR NOTES

It is always a pleasure to be able to thank those who have helped make this journey remarkable. First, my readers. You asked for Rhoane's story and I hope I didn't disappoint. He has more tales to tell, I'm sure of it.

I also want to thank Abel Fetter and Karol Inskeep for their insightful beta reads. They know how to keep me striving to write the best story possible. To Carly O'Donoghue for challenging me to heed the villain's call. And to Callene Rapp, what can I say? I love you. So, so much. Thank you for taking the time away from your own writing to help with this book.

And to my wonderful editor Faith Williams of The Atwater Group, thank you. Any and all typos are mine and mine alone. Faith is amazing at polishing my words, but sometimes I add a scuff here and there. If you find any errors, please email me to let me know. Your enjoyment of my books is the most important thing.

Thank you to Carol Phillips, Anna Spies, and Renflowergrapx for their gorgeous maps and interior artwork. Daqri Combs at Covers by Combs made the gorgeous covers you now see on the entire series. Thank you.

As always, thank you to my David. He is my very own prince charming.

ABOUT THE AUTHOR

Tameri Etherton is a *USA Today* Bestselling and award-winning author of fierce scorching fantasy and paranormal romance. She grew up inventing fictional worlds where the impossible was possible.

It's been said she leaves a trail of glitter in her wake as she creates new adventures for her kickass heroines, and the rogues who steal their hearts.

She lives an enchanted life traveling the world with her very own prince charming and their mischievous dragon, Lady Dazzleton.

Read More from Tameri Etherton and explore the Aetherverse at
www.TameriEtherton.com